HANGING AT COMANCHE WELLS

Three determined men—an old judge, a weary sheriff and a worried young man—were all that stood between the hired killer and the powerful Cattlemen's Association that wanted their personal gunman free.

The Cattlemen's Association had paid for and alibi'd half-a-dozen cold-blooded killings. Then their executioner had gotten out of hand and wantonly murdered for his own pleasure, sure he could count on his well-placed friends to save him . . . and he could.

HANGING AT COMANCHE WELLS

Benjamin Capps

GUNSMOKE
TOPEKA & SHAWNEE COUNTY
PUBLIC LIBRARY
TOPEKA KANSAS

This hardback edition 2001
by Chivers Press
by arrangement with
Golden West Literary Agency

ISBN 0 7540 8142 7

British Library Cataloguing in Publication Data available

Printed and bound in Great Britain by
Bookcraft, Midsomer Norton, Somerset

Chapter 1

DEPUTY YOUNGBLOOD came out of the new Carroll County courthouse, elbowed his way through the crowd of waiting cattlemen and townspeople, and headed down main street. Most of the stores were closed, and the broad dusty street was empty of people, but along the hitchrails were tied many saddle horses and rigs of all kinds, light hacks and buckboards with thin wheels, freight wagons and even one covered chuck wagon with heavy wide wheels. Ranchers from thirty miles away were in town; spring roundup was over. From the horse brands, it seemed that all the boys from the Rail-P were there. Some of the men were in town ostensibly after supplies, but all of them were there actually for the same thing, the trial.

Funny, he thought, how they all took it for granted what the verdict would be, yet they all wanted to hear it. He supposed it was human nature to want to be around when something happens, so you can have your say about it, and afterwards shoot the bull about it as a man who was there.

The business buildings along the street had tall square false fronts with the names of the proprietors painted on them in heavy letters; some of the stores had covered board walks, others nothing but dirt in front of them, so that as Youngblood went down the west side of the street he walked alternately in the shade and in the sun, stepping up out of the alkali dust onto the planks and then back down to the dirt again. Some of the buildings were in good repair, painted white or blue or barn red; others, never painted, were the dark gray color of weathered pine lumber, the weather stripping of their walls running vertically in the manner of backwoods buildings of the South, whence came a part of the tradition of Comanche Wells. The largest building in town was the

5

B

Robert Lee Hotel; it sported a second-storey gallery, half in the manner of a Spanish balcony, with fancy wooden balustrade. The town scattered out from the one main street to cover fifty acres, sparsely. To the south was a growth of squat adobe huts, like a part of the bare flats where they sat, their dark doors and windows a contrast to their light-colored moulded walls. To the east, out past the livery stables, lay a scattering of plank shacks, mostly with one room. Out to the west by itself among the tall cottonwood trees was the big white house of Stephen Pendergrass.

The deputy turned in at the White Plaza Saloon but saw that the door was locked and carried a sign reading "Open Tonight." McSween's, down three blocks, would probably be open; McSween wouldn't risk losing a nickel in trade to see a murder trial. Anyway, Youngblood knew he'd better go check because the sheriff's main reason for sending him on the rounds of main street was to find out what, if anything, was going on in the saloons and to lay down a little law to the proprietors.

It might possibly be the last rounds he'd ever make. If they brought in the verdict and turned Ivey loose this afternoon, things should be quiet and peaceful again in a few days. The "rounds" were a ritual instituted by the sheriff long before the trial, just shortly after they had taken Ivey into custody. "Go around town and see what everybody's talking about," he would say. "See what's going on." It wasn't because the sheriff was a practical politician, which he was, but because the whole business of Ivey and the Cattlemen's Association and the murder of a twelve-year-old boy, a sheepman's son, was a ticklish deal; and the sheriff knew that himself and three deputies were precious few to control the angry forces that could arise out of it.

When it did quieten down and become peaceful again, Deputy Youngblood had a minor shock for the sheriff; he was ready to turn in his badge. No one knew it yet except him and his wife; he had definitely decided to give in to her and go back to a ranch job. It wasn't just to please her, though he would have done it for that with her in the condition she was, but because her arguments had begun to get through to him. Life in a place like this was rough enough without borrowing all the trouble

6

of the mixed-up elements, the ranchers, big and small, with different ideas, the sheep herders, the farmers, the land speculators, the free-range hogs, the fence cutters, the range burners, Yankee and Southern sympathizers, greasers and gringos. How simple it would be, he thought, to wear a gun if you wore it just to defend yourself and your family and what you knew was worth defending. The trouble with the deputy job was that he couldn't quit when he wanted to, even if his wife was going crazy with worry and regardless of her condition. This whole damned Ivey deal was a good example; the sheriff had been shorthanded through it all, and any deputy that quit would have been named a coward by both sides. One thing, Lila had been understanding about that part; he could hear her quaint words: "I mean get out of it when you can with honor." He would not have used the words "with honor," but they expressed the meaning well enough.

In passing the small white building which housed the town's newspaper, the *Courier,* a movement in the doorway caught his eye and he turned to see the editor, Ezra Pitts, who had come to the door to examine in the better light a strip of paper.

The editor saw him at the same time and called, "Oh, Mr. Youngblood, would you have a minute to spare?"

He laughed. "Well, maybe one minute. How come you're not at the trial? Isn't that news?"

"Well, for one thing I was down there a while ago, and I couldn't get in. People around here don't seem to have enough respect for the press. Another thing, I've got to get out a paper tomorrow. Will they bring in the verdict this afternoon?"

"Ought to be before long," he told the editor. "The sheriff got a message the jury was ready, and he was going to escort them back to the courthouse. Which reminds me, I got to be going."

"Wait, say, Mr. Youngblood, would have time to read this proof and see if I've made any bloopers?" Mr. Pitts looked serious. He was a small man dressed in a white shirt and tie and he seemed to always wear a dirty black apron and always take himself seriously.

"Bloopers?"

"Yes, you know, well, I'm still more or less a dude,

7

you might say. This is a very serious thing, and I just don't want to say something that would make a true westerner, you might say, laugh. The press can be a powerful instrument, Mr. Youngblood, if it's taken seriously. Watch the ink. It's still wet."

The proof was headed, "LAW AND ORDER — WHEN? An Editorial Concerning the Recent Trial of One William Ivey, a Paid Killer." The text read,

"Yesterday the District Court sitting in Comanche Wells turned Free a man who is Admitted by one and all, including Himself, to be a Paid Killer by profession. His career has been a varied and Spotted one, but since his discharge as a detective for the local Cattlemens' Association he has been in the employ of a Party or Parties Unknown, deliberately building a Reputation as a heartless Back-Shooter of Cattle Rustlers, thus trying by entirely illegal means to bring this so-called Rustling to an end. But can we bring Law and Order to our Locality by these Means? The answer is NO.

"The trial had all the Appearance of Legality and Propriety but was known to be a Farce by this Fact: that the verdict was Known by all the Good People of this Town when the said William Ivey was first taken into Custody and even Before the so-called Trial began. The Accused has made his Name known from East Texas to the Territory of New Mexico and from the Indian Territory to the furtherest southern extent of our great Country, and it is said that he cannot be convicted of any Crime where the primary Industry is the raising of Cattle, but let all Concerned consider This: Can Law and Order be thus Flouted and still remain of any Force at all?

"We of the COURIER are not Concerned Primarily with the question of Ivey's guilt or Innocence in the sordid killing of a twelve-year-old boy, which he denies. But we Do most heartily Deplore the public Apathy which causes us to Submit to the existence of such a Paid Killer and the Public

8

Opinion which seems Among some Citizens to make a Hero of said Paid Killer. We of the COURIER will be found on the side of Constituted Authority and will continue to do what we are Able to rouse our well appreciated readers and advertisers against such rascals as William Ivey."

When Deputy Youngblood had read the strip of newsprint, he studied the little editor, who had an innocent questioning look on his face, and asked him, "You mean you figure to print this in your paper tomorrow?"

"Yes. I thought I'd put it in the center of page one and put a heavy black border around it."

"What was that you wanted to know about? Bloopers?" Youngblood laughed. "This whole thing is a blooper, Pitts. You've got your loop over a mountain lion here, and he can't go anywhere but straight at you. I wouldn't print it."

"Not print it? Surely a law officer like yourself must be in favor of law and order, Mr. Youngblood. I'm afraid you don't understand the function of a newspaper. This is an editorial, and it certainly is our duty to print our honest opinions and try to shed some light . . ."

"Maybe," Youngblood interrupted him, "you are the one who doesn't understand."

"What? How's that?"

"Well, there's a lot you don't understand, but let's just take that 'farce' word. The trial is on the square, and I don't think Judge Pendergrass is going to appreciate you saying it's not."

Editor Pitt's eyes lit up at this. "Then tell me. Why is it everybody says, 'Oh, they'll let him go; they'll never convict him'? How is it that everybody already knows?"

Youngblood laughed at him again. "Well, what are *you* saying? How do *you* know? Maybe they're all like you and believe everything they hear." He turned to go, then stopped and asked, "Isn't Mr. Pendergrass, Stephen Pendergrass, interested in this paper?"

The editor replied belligerently, "What's that got to do with it? I'm the editor and publisher. I write the editorials. Money doesn't buy any space in the *Courier's* editorial columns."

"Don't get on your high horse, Pitts," Youngblood said.

9

"I'm just trying to save you from a busted nose or maybe a bullet hole through your head. If Mr. Pendergrass is interested in the paper, talk to him about it. I guarantee he can tell you plenty you don't know. He can tell you dern near everything that's happened in this town and in this state since they took it away from the Indians."

Editor Pitts said, "But I happen to have information that Mr. Pendergrass is prejudiced. He has cattle connections."

Youngblood laughed again but without much feeling of mirth. "God, Pitts!" he said, "you're like some month-old calf in a stampede. Cattle connections! You think Pendergrass is a banker? He just owns that bank to keep his money in. You look out west of this town, and far as you can see across that flat prairie belongs to Mr. Pendergrass. Cattle connections! Mr. Pendergrass owns the Rail-P, and if you'll just count the Rail-P brands strung out along those hitching rails out there, maybe you'll believe me when I say it's the biggest spread in a hundred miles of here." He went out shaking his head. "Don't print it, Pitts. Find out what you're talking about first."

Heading on down the street he met the man they had spoken of, Mr. Pendergrass, a large, proud old man whose given name was Stephen F., said by some to be the first boy born of Anglo-Saxon parents in Texas. He was *the* Mr. Pendergrass of Comanche Wells, though he had a brother who was a traveling judge and who held regular court in the town since the new courthouse had been finished. Youngblood thought at first that he would mention something about Editor Pitt's editorial, but realized immediately that it was none of his business and that his interference might cause more trouble than the ignorant editor's ideas. He said, "Howdy, Mr. Pendergrass," and the old man nodded slightly as they passed.

He found McSween's open as he had thought it would be and went in. McSween was sweeping the floor. Youngblood said, "Looks like I caught you working, Mack."

"Yeah, I haven't got no help these days," McSween said. "I can't keep them away from that courthouse." He leaned on his broom. Sweat was rolling off his forehead and down his fat cheeks. He wore a baggy white shirt and a small black bow tie that was almost lost under his heavy jowls. "How about a drink?"

"No thanks," Youngblood said. "I'm working. You know the sheriff is kind of particular about that."

"The sheriff won't never hear about it from me," the bartender said.

"Thanks anyway. I just came in to talk to you about tonight."

"What about tonight?" McSween was suspicious. "I figured on doing a pretty good run of business tonight."

"I wouldn't be surprised if you did," Youngblood told him. "But the sheriff's office would appreciate it if you would watch the fellers pretty close tonight. You know, if anybody's getting high or making trouble you can refuse to serve him or even throw him out. Me or Slim or somebody will be around to back you up if you have a big crowd."

The bartender had begun to splutter. "Hell's fire! Youngblood, tonight it looks like I might sell more whisky than I ever sold before, and you tell me to throw my customers out or not serve them. What's wrong with a man making a decent living around here?"

"You remember last winter when the sheriff sent me after that horsethief?" Youngblood asked calmly. "I chased him clear up to Tascosa before I caught him. Well, anyway, I just wanted to tell you about a little trouble they had up there at Tascosa the night I got in. They had turned some feller out of jail, and he was holding a celebration in a saloon. Things got real gay, and then real rough, and they knocked over a couple of lamps and got coal oil all over the floor. Well, when it was all finished, McSween, that saloon was burnt clear down level with the ground."

McSween looked sad.

"We just don't want anybody killed tonight. You know there's a lot of feeling against Ivey around here and a lot of feeling in favor of him. And the trouble is people on either side of it don't agree among themselves. If he comes in here tonight and you get a big crowd, you're going to be sitting on a powder barrel."

"It may be kind of hard to refuse to serve Ivey," the bartender said. "He's going to be thirsty after setting in jail all this time."

"Don't refuse Ivey. Let him drink all he wants."

"You mean you don't want nobody drunk but Ivey?"

11

"That's about the size of it," Youngblood chuckled. "I don't guess anything would please the sheriff better than to have Ivey get drunk right away, plum stone cold drunk, and spend the night passed out and get up tomorrow with the biggest hangover he ever had and then get on a horse and ride out of here."

He left McSween's place thinking that the man would probably cooperate, for whatever that would be worth. Heading back up the street toward the courthouse, he wondered whether he would have time to go over home and see how Lila was feeling, or more important to let her know everything was all right. She was apt to worry. He couldn't see any particular movement at the courthouse that would indicate the trial had turned out, but, of course, that didn't mean it might not happen any minute. He decided to wait and if the sheriff wanted him tonight, which he would, he would say he had to go home to supper.

A half block from the small *Courier* building, he heard loud, angry voices and quickened his pace. As he clomped across the board walk in front of the Alamo Groceries and Provisions Co., he saw Mr. Pendergrass stride out of the newspaper office. The old man, walking as tall and proud as a general in front of his troops, fixed Deputy Youngblood with a gaze of meaningless fury, then wheeled and strode up the street toward the bank.

Youngblood heard what seemed a moan of pain from the newspaper office. He ran in and found, behind the front office partition, Editor Pitts in an extreme state of consternation, staring aghast at a mess of metal type strung out on the floor.

"Look at it!" the editor moaned. "Look at it! My beautiful editorial!" And to Youngblood, "Why couldn't he discuss it? What is he? An animal of some kind?"

"Did Mr. Pendergrass spill your type?" Youngblood asked.

"Spill it? He threw it! Like he was God himself! He wouldn't discuss it with me!"

"Well, can't you pick it up and put it together again?" Youngblood asked, trying to keep from grinning. It wasn't very funny anyway, but highhanded and uncalled for. He would have offered to help pick up the scattered type if he had had time.

"Pick it up and put it together?" the editor moaned.

"It's pied! Can't you see it's pied? It'll take me two weeks in my spare time to sort it out again. But I'll set that editorial up again tonight. Don't you worry about that." He began to shake his inky forefinger in Youngblood's face. "I'll set the editorial up again, and this time it'll scorch his ears when he reads it. Don't you worry about that!"

Youngblood backed out of the office, grinning openly now. It might be, he thought, that if the editor was wild and silly enough no one would take him seriously.

When he got out the door, he could hear a new commotion at the courthouse. The waiting crowd of men had spilled out into the broad street and were yelling to one another. There was a strange note of disbelief in the voices, as if something had gone wrong. He could not make out any words, but he hurried toward the scene.

The new courthouse was a long two-storey building made of small rough native stone, the roof gabled at one end where the jail was and hipped at the other, with five stone chimneys sticking up out of the shingles. It had upper and lower galleries in the center at the front, and wooden stairways rose to the upper gallery from both sides. Toward the rear were toilets, a corral and barn where the sheriff kept horses, and a covered well. Now, out of the door at the upper gallery, men were coming, crowding down the stairs at either side. One of Pendergrass' bank clerks, a pale skinny man, burst out of the melee and came toward Youngblood running. The deputy called to him, "What happened? What's the matter?" and, seeing that the clerk did not intend to stop, he blocked his path and repeated, "What's wrong? What happened?"

The clerk was dodging to get past, like a boy playing tag, but his face showed fright. "Guilty!" he panted. "They found Ivey guilty!"

Chapter 2

THE SHERIFF'S OFFICE was a 15-by-20 front room on the ground floor of the jail end of the courthouse. It had a

13

flat-top desk and a roll-top desk, two wooden file cabinets, a swivel chair and several straight chairs, a rack full of rifles, and a pot-bellied wood stove which sat gathering dust. The walls were littered with tacked up wanted and reward posters of yellowed cardboard or paper, curling at the corners.

The place was crowded; one of Ivey's dude lawyers was there, the county clerk, the other two deputies, and a juryman who was talking to the sheriff. Youngblood wondered whether he could get away for an hour without being missed. He saw that Slim and Andy, the other two deputies, seemed to be waiting for something, so he decided he'd better ask the sheriff about it. He spoke in a low voice to Slim. "So William Ivey's guilty, huh?"

"Yeah. Don't that beat it? I never thought they had the guts."

"How did Ivey take it?"

"He was still laughing when we put him in a cell upstairs."

"Anybody tried to make any trouble?"

"Not yet, but there was plenty of talk."

The juryman left. Youngblood spoke hurriedly, thinking that the county clerk might be about to tie up the sheriff in a long talk.

"I'm going to run home, Sheriff. I'll be back in an hour or so."

"What for?" the sheriff asked. He was a middle-aged man, built like a brick building, who spoke directly to the point and was seldom found at a loss about what to do.

"Why, to eat supper," Youngblood said.

"How about staying here? Maggie will bring something in."

"Well, I got another reason too, Sheriff. Sort of personal. I really ought to go by home a couple of minutes."

The sheriff was a fair man to work for, in spite of being gruff and direct sometimes. He said, "Could it wait a while? The judge wants to speak to us, Youngblood. Then you can go, but I'd like you to spend the night here if you can."

The bank clerk whom Youngblood had stopped out in the street appeared at the open office door. He still

14

looked frightened. He knocked and came in and spoke to the sheriff. "I'm looking for the judge."

"What for?" the sheriff asked.

"I got a message for him. An urgent message."

"You might try his office," the sheriff said. "The front door of the courthouse isn't locked."

"He's not in his office."

"He's in the building. Wait here if you want to. He'll be in right away." The sheriff began to talk to the lawyer and the county clerk.

After a few minutes Judge Pendergrass came in through the door to the hall. "Hello, Youngblood," he said. "How's your wife?"

"Hello, Judge. Fine. She's fine."

The judge spoke to Andy and Slim, calling them by name. The most noticeable feature of the judge was his crippled leg, not so much the fact of the leg being bad, as the remarkable manner in which he could get about. Without a crutch or other aid he walked in great strides, swaying from side to side and up and down, from the shortness of the game leg. He was smaller than his brother, *the* Mr. Pendergrass, but had the same Roman nose, slightly hooked, and the same deep-set eyes, now and then magnified by his brass-rimmed spectacles. There was a difference in the faces, and it came from the fact that the judge's face seemed much alive when he talked, and crowfoot wrinkles showed at the corners of his eyes.

The bank clerk came forward. "Judge, Mr. Pendergrass wants to see you."

"Hello, Peters," the judge said. "What does Stephen want to see me about?"

"Why, that's a private matter, Judge. He just wants to see you right away."

"Right away, huh?" The crowfoot marks appeared at the corners of the judge's eyes. "Well, I tell you, I'm pretty busy right now. Ask Mr. Pendergrass if he'll please come around to my office tomorrow."

"Oh, I think Mr. Pendergrass means for you to come down to the bank. And today."

"And you think I'd better come right down there whether I'm busy or not, do you?"

"Well, I don't think Mr. Pendergrass would have sent

15

for you if it wasn't important, and if he didn't mean for you to come right away."

The sheriff said, "You want me to throw this feller out of here, Judge?"

"I guess not," the judge laughed. "Mr. Peters, you work for my brother Stephen, so when he told you to bring me a message, you hit the trail and brought me the message. But I don't work for my brother. Please tell him that I won't have time to come to the bank, nor to see him at all today."

The clerk stared at everyone, amazed, and left shaking his head as if to say that now he'd seen everything.

The dude lawyer smiled suavely during the laughter about the clerk, then said, "Judge Pendergrass, there's one matter I'd like to ask you about informally, though with due respect, of course."

"What's that?"

"Why did your honor set the date for the execution of the sentence? Or perhaps I should ask if your honor wouldn't consider it somewhat irregular to specify the date in the face of a notice of appeal?"

"Not so irregular as to make any difference, Counselor. I had my reason, and you may as well know it: this case is not going to drag on and on. It's going to be settled before August the first."

"But surely your honor is aware that the effect of the appeal is to suspend the proceedings in the district court."

"Well, Counselor, I've answered your 'informal' question about as well as I can. I guarantee that you have all the time you need. I know how the court of criminal appeals works. And I also guarantee you that the higher court will allow no delay, and unless your appeal is successful, your client will hang on August the first.

"I'm glad for the chance to speak to you out of court, though," the judge went on, "because I have something else to say. You know as well as I do that it may prejudice your client's appeal if there is any violence such as an attempted jail break. What you may not know is that some such violence is quite possible, even probable. You've heard some talk, I'm sure; now don't discount that talk too much, Counselor. Some men in this part of the state today are accustomed to using violence to get their way; it seems more natural to them than a legal appeal. I understand that the Cattlemen's Association meets tomorrow. If I were you I would be at that meeting, and I would make the facts plain to them: any illegal action in Ivey's behalf is going to prejudice his appeal."

The lawyer's smile had faded while the judge was talking. He had evidently planned to have the upper hand in the conversation; now he seemed to want no more of it; the verdict had been hard on his self-confidence. He half bowed to the sheriff and the deputies, thanked the judge, and went out the door with as much grace as he could muster. The judge was equally polite to him, but it was clear as he turned back to the other four men in the room that his feelings about the smooth, well-dressed lawyer were similiar to theirs.

"Why don't you set down, Judge," the sheriff said.

"Thank you, no. I can think better standing up. But go ahead; let's don't stand on any ceremony, gentlemen." The word "gentlemen" did not sound out of place coming from the judge; he had a way of making himself at home. The four lawmen were dressed in plaid shirts, stockmen's boots, pants that you could ride a horse in, guns and gunbelts that had a worn business-like look about them, and wide-brimmed hats pushed to the backs of their heads. The judge was dressed in a gray cotton suit, rumpled and cool looking, but he gave the impression that he belonged.

"You don't have anyone in the cell behind the office?" he asked.

The sheriff shook his head.

"We just want to keep this private. Gentlemen, I appreciate the sheriff letting me talk to you. I've got several things to say and the first one is kind of ticklish. I hope nobody takes offence, but it's a matter of loyalty. I make a pretty good example myself; I've got a brother here who's one of the oldest and most respected ranchers around. Well, a while ago one of his swampers was in here, you know, and expected me to run right down to the bank to see him. I don't know what he wants with me, but I do know that he doesn't want Ivey to hang. Who knows? He might ask me to do something I shouldn't do. Well, if he does, he's due for a disappointment.

"You see I've dedicated my life to the law. I don't

17

mean anything fancy by that; I just mean that I've worked hard to qualify myself to do a job I think is important. Then I sought this judgeship, and it has been intrusted to me. Now I think I ought to do the best I can or get out of it, and the day some other loyalty comes first with me, I will get out of it. It's not a matter of being disloyal to my brother. He has a bank here in Comanche Wells; I wouldn't ask him to run off with all his depositors' money, and he has no right to ask me to do anything but my plain duty as a judge."

The sheriff broke in. "Why, Judge, you don't have to tell us that. You're the last word in honesty, and nobody around here has got a bit of doubt about it." He looked at his deputies as if to say he could whip the man who doubted it.

"Well, thank you," the judge chuckled. "I was sort of thinking of myself as an *example,* but I did want to say where I stand. You see, I've got a couple of ideas we ought to hash over, and then I think we'll see that this Ivey deal is more critical than a man might first think. But before we hash over these ideas, we've got to be satisfied about the loyalty matter. It's important; take my word for it. No lawman is going to sit on the fence. They're going to try to bribe us, threaten us, persuade us, and in the end they'll use guns against us. I don't believe I can make it any clearer than that. If any one of us is not willing to do his job, the time to quit is now. And I don't mean next week; I mean now."

The little judge had been leaning against the rifle rack, his game leg propped up over his good one. He gave himself a little push which seemed about to cause him to fall forward on his face but which instead propelled him into his remarkable swaying stride. He swung to the other end of the room, then returned and stopped in front of Youngblood, who was leaning against the wall.

"You can count on these boys, Judge," the sheriff said. Evidently the problem still didn't seem as complicated to him as it did to the judge.

"We're behind you, Judge," Slim said, grinning.

"We'll stick, Judge," Andy said.

"I wouldn't blame any man that quit now," the judge said. "Right now. Two weeks from now if he quit, I'd figure he was a traitor. Youngblood, you were raised on a ranch; what do you say?"

Youngblood was thinking about something different from what the judge implied, about Lila and not about some supposed loyalty to ranching interests. "I got nothing to hide," he said slowly. "You all know Charlie Moss is my uncle, and he owns the Circle-2, but I don't think you'll find him bucking the law. Funny thing, though." He turned to the sheriff. "I was going to quit you as soon as they turned Ivey loose and things quieted down. I figured to turn in my badge tomorrow or the next day."

The sheriff was surprised. "What's the matter, Youngblood? Hell, I figured you was happy as a hog in a mudhole. What's the beef? Maybe we can straighten it out."

"No beef," he lied. "I worked as rep for Uncle Charlie, and one year I bossed his roundup crew when old Bill Kelsey was sick. Well, old Bill is getting old to ride all day, and Uncle Charlie figures I can handle the regular foreman's job, so I was going to give it a whirl."

No one spoke for a minute, then the judge said, "Why were you going to wait until they turned Ivey loose and things quieted down?"

It occurred to Youngblood that the judge could see right through him. God! how could you say, my wife wants me to quit because the work's too dangerous, and I'm going to do what she wants, because she's going to have a kid and she's kind of scared about it, and she depends on me. Then suddenly it occurred to him as he stared into the deep-set eyes of the little judge that he really didn't have anything to hide, that the judge would back him up, and that he actually had brass enough to say it; except that he didn't want to. He had meant to work for the sheriff as long as he was needed, and the only difference now was that he would be needed another month. That damned simple.

"How bad do you need me?" he asked the sheriff.

"I need you real bad."

"I'll stay," he said to the sheriff, and to the judge, "I'll do my job."

"That's good enough for me," the judge said.

"Now let's go into this appeal," he went on. "Gentlemen, the appeal will be denied. I know the justices of the court in Austin who will hear this appeal; I sat in a law office about six years with one of them. I know the particular principles that they will judge it by. There is no substantial error in the case, and the appeal will be denied. Now, this means two things. First, it gives us time; they don't know it and we do. That gives us time to plan. You know, if Ivey was scheduled to hang tomorrow, there would be a mob of ranchers in here tonight and they would tear out the end of this building if they had to to get him out. But they don't know but what the appeal may work, and they may hold off. The second thing it means to us is this: we know what we're up against. We've got a man to hang on the first of August, and no appeal court is going to give us an easy out."

While the judge was speaking a pounding noise began upstairs and toward the rear of the building. The sheriff said, "I'm not goint to put up with much of that. Slim, go up and tell that guy to act decent. Take your gun off first."

A minute later Slim was back, grinning. "Ivey says he don't like that cell; it's too little. Says he can't get enough exercise. And he says besides that he's starving; says he had a hard day in court. I told him he'd get some chow when Maggie got it ready."

The pounding started again, clearer because Slim had the door into the hall open.

The sheriff showed his irritation. "You tell that guy," he said to Slim, "he's in the cell where he's going to stay, and when we take him out we're going to exercise his neck. If he wants decent treatment he can act decent. I'll come up there and lay him out with a gunbutt."

A minute later Slim was back with a still bigger grin on his face. "Ivey says you come on up there and take your gun off, and he'll whup you all over that cell."

The sheriff rose and started unbuckling his gunbelt. He wore a forty-eight inch belt and didn't have any sag in his stomach. Then his eyes met those of the judge, and he slowly slid back into his big oak chair. "I'll take his supper up when it comes," he said, "and I'll find out if he wants to cooperate or if he wants to raise cane. I'm sorry about the interruption, Judge. Go on. Close the door, Slim."

"Well, I thought there was just one more thing we need to run over," the judge said. "You all heard parts of the trial, and you've heard rumors, and so on; but how well

20

do we all agree about what Ivey's been doing the last few years? How much of it can we pin down?"

The sheriff said, "I think everybody around here knows what Ivey's been doing. He's been bushwacking guys he thought was rustlers, at six-hundred dollars a head."

"That's pretty near the point I was getting at," the judge said. "But we know part of the rumors were false. Ivey got credit for killing a man on a trail herd clear up in Kansas when he was in jail in El Paso for another killing."

"Well, I brought him in for the Brown killing," the sheriff said, "and he had an alibi that held up, but I always figured he was guilty anyway."

"I heard him bragging right down here in the White Plaza Saloon one night," Andy put in, "and he was showing his rifle. He had fourteen notches cut in the stock."

Youngblood said, "I always figured that was part of his scheme, the bragging. Sure, he killed some men, but he was trying to put the fear of God into a bunch of others, and he always claimed more killings than he did."

"Well, let's pin it down," the judge said. "We know that Ivey was working for the Cattlemen's Association here three or four years ago as a stock detective. He went away out south of here into the Blue Mule Mountains, and he brought in three men for rustling. He brought in a pack saddle full of hides and branding irons and stuff for evidence, and he also brought in a Mexican and another cowpuncher for witnesses. He took them over to Jefferson City, and a jury over there turned them loose. I've seen the records on that trial. A short time after that Ivey talked to a Cattlemen's Association meeting here in Comanche Wells; I'm talking about the meeting when he got fired or quit, whichever it was. That would have been . . . what? Three years ago, Youngblood?"

"Yes sir, they were already starting to plan the spring roundup, so it must have been about April, just over three years ago."

"I understand that you were at that meeting, Youngblood."

"Yes sir."

"What did Ivey have to say?"

"Well, of course he was pretty bitter, Judge. First, I

21

remember he told them there wasn't any real big rustling operations, just a bunch of little ones; one head, ten head, no more than twenty head at a time. It was just a matter of everybody eating beef whether they had any cows or not, or trying to build up a little herd, or maybe selling a few head to the Indians. It was just enough to take all the profit out of ranching. Well, everybody knew that was about the way it was, but when Ivey said he knew how to stop it, and the only way to stop it, then everybody get real interested.

"He said it would just take one man with a rifle. He said if he was going to do it he would pick out some feller that was known by his neighbors to be a rustler, some feller that wasn't too well liked anyway, and leave him a warning note that he was going to be killed for rustling. Let the word get around about this warning, and then hide out and shoot the feller in the back."

"Did you notice what anybody in particular said about it?" the judge asked.

"No sir, there was a lot of muttering an jawing, but the only thing I heard right then was somebody asked Ivey why not call the rustler out face to face and kill him. Ivey said a rustler didn't deserve a chance, and it would do a lot more good if he was shot in the back when he didn't expect it. About that time, Bledsoe—he was president of the Association that year—began to pound his gavel and said maybe they shouldn't take up any such question as that. And there was three or four more that said they shouldn't discuss it."

"Now wait," the judge said. "Those three or four men; probably some of them meant it shouldn't be discussed at all, but maybe one of them meant it shouldn't be discussed *then* and *there*. Could you put your finger on the exact thing that was said by any certain man?"

Youngblood paused to think. "No, Judge, I couldn't. I know Ivey said he wasn't going to work for the Association like he had been, and that just about broke up the meeting. I remember what Charlie Moss said about it; he said things had come to a pretty pass when men would sit around and talk about bushwhacking."

"Well, that just about completes the circumstantial evidence," the judge said. "In the next eighteen months, five men were killed this side of Fort Worth, at least five, according to the pattern that Ivey had laid down. Wouldn't you say that Brown was killed according to Ivey's plan, Sheriff? He was doing a little rustling, wasn't he?"

"Yes, I would," the sheriff said. "Not much doubt about it."

"Well, Brown wasn't the first. A man named Dudley up close to Briggsburg was first. Now, here's the point of all this: sometime between that Association meeting and the time Dudley was killed, somebody took Ivey up on that plan. Ivey's no cattleman; he wouldn't have done it on his own; besides that, he's had plenty of money without doing any work that anybody could tell. So, we're not dealing with any rumor. Some party or parties unknown is in this, besides Ivey, and if I was that party, I would be pretty nervous right now about Ivey's hanging."

The sheriff said, "You're thinking Ivey might talk."

"Yes, but more than that I'm thinking that this party can't afford to take a chance that he might. There are a bunch of cattlemen around here that are sympathetic to Ivey, and we don't know how far they'll go, but this unknown party is going to be planning and scheming every minute and he's going as far as he's got to go. Ivey is the sort of man who would talk just for revenge if he figured his backer didn't stick by him."

The judge had sat down, his game leg sticking out stiff at the side of the chair. Now he stood and pushed the brass-rimmed spectacles up on his nose. "Well, gentlemen, I've certainly done enough gabbing for one night, but I think it has been worth our time. I believe we all understand what we face. I have a feeling in my bones that we will come through this matter all right, and I'll say this: I don't know any four men I'd rather be in it with than you all right here. And now, I'd better get along; I have some paperwork to get done tonight."

He was at the office front door about the time when the timid knock came. He opened it to see the young colored boy who worked around the home of Stephen Pendergrass. The boy backed up with his hat in his hand and said, "Mr. Pendergrass wants the pleasure of yo company for supper, Mr. Jedge."

"Well, Remus, I've already sent him a message that I

would be busy," the judge said. "Didn't he get my message?"

"I think so, Mr. Jedge, but he wants you to come on and come out there anyway."

"Well, I'm just very sorry, Remus, but I won't be able to make it."

"I shore do hate to hear you say that, Mr. Jedge, because Mr. Pendergrass is all tore up, and I'm afraid he going to whale the tar out of me if you don't come on to supper."

"Oh, I don't think he would do that, Remus. Please tell Mr. Pendergrass that I am sorry to decline the invitation."

The colored boy left mumbling, "he sorry to decline," as if he were memorizing some words that he expected to use later. The judge followed shortly after.

Chapter 3

WHEN YOUNGBLOOD left the jail and headed for home it was dusk. He walked slowly, though the sheriff had said, "Make it a short hour. We may need you." He figured that was the way it was going to be all this coming month: hurry up and get back to business, every night away from home. It would be harder on Lila than it would on him, because of the waiting. Maybe it would be better just to take her out to the ranch and leave her until it was all over.

His house sat on a half block of city land, and the land alone had cost him a hundred and twenty dollars. There was room for a garden and a saddle horse and milk cow. He had gotten rid of the milk cow because Lila would chase all over the town bog looking for the critter when he wasn't there to do it himself. She was still working the garden this summer even though he had forbidden her.

She was waiting in the front doorway for him. She kissed him and said, "I waited and waited, and you didn't come, so I threw your supper out."

24

"I'll bet you did, you stingy little thing," he said. "If I hadn't come home till morning, you'd still have my supper waiting."

She was a black-haired girl, six years younger than Bart Youngblood, and he had never quite gotten over his surprise at having won her. Then partly it was the difference in their ages that made him feel as he did, protective, more than he needed to be. The fact that she had proven again and again not to be so young and helpless as he supposed did not change this attitude in him, but added to it a sense of wonder at her, as if through her innocence she gained some secret power. The way she held her body now that she was grown clumsy in the last weeks of pregnancy roused in him this protectiveness and wonder. She held herself straight, without apology, with a kind of simple impudence. He would not have had her act any other way; certainly there was no shame in bearing his child. But sometimes he felt like crying out to her, "God, Lila! Little Lila, don't trust me to make it all easy for you." And then he could picture her in the suffering of long labor, when he wouldn't be able to do anything, and imagine her cruelly losing her trust in whatever it was she trusted in. But of course it was useless thinking, and foolish too. He himself had been born in a buffalo hunter's tent, as he had heard his uncle tell many times, without a doctor within forty miles, and probably with no woman other than his mother within forty miles unless it were an Indian squaw. He had been born in a dry camp, just upwind from a half acre of buffalo hides pegged out in the sun. Still the common sense of the matter did not rule his feelings; common sense was good enough in every other thing he thought about, but not when he thought about Lila.

When he had hung his gunbelt on a nail and started to wash up, she said, "You needn't be worrying about breaking the news to me. Mrs. Ainslee was over. She says they sentenced William Ivey to hang."

"That's right," he said, spewing as he scooped the water from the pan onto his face.

"What does it mean, Bart?"

"Nothing much, to us. It just means the sheriff will need me another month. But that job with Uncle Charlie will wait."

"One month?" she asked, as if it were important.

"Sure, just one month. August the first; that's the date."

"August the first!"

"Yes. What's the matter, Lila? What's wrong with that, just one more month?"

She had turned away from him. "It doesn't really matter. Of course it doesn't. How could that matter?" She managed a weak laugh. "It's just that ... It's my time; that's what Doc said: August the first."

He thought it over a minute and then said, "I'm getting you out of here, out to the ranch, where it's quieter. And away from all these town gossips."

While he ate she was gay, as if to reassure him, and when he was getting ready to leave, she said, "It doesn't matter, really, about the date. Doctors are never right about the date anyway."

"I won't worry if you won't," he said. "I'll be back when I can."

"Be careful," she said.

The sheriff had made some plans. A good many of the cattlemen and their hands were still in town, and all of them were drinking. They might try something brash tonight, before they got the word from the dude lawyer. It wouldn't be much of a jailbreak attempt; they wouldn't be organized enough, but it was worth watching for. He sent Andy across the street with a rifle to station himself on top of the hardware store, but cautioned him, "Don't shoot anybody if you can get around it."

Youngblood and Slim he sent upstairs to wait in the windows overlooking the street. "One of you can sleep if you want to, but make sure you know which one is supposed to be sleeping," he cautioned. "And stay away from Ivey's cell with a gun."

Youngblood and Slim pulled a steel army cot out of a cell and carried it into the front room where there were two unbarred windows. No sound came from Ivey's cell, and Youngblood wondered how the condemned prisoner could sleep; perhaps he was just lying there thinking, but Ivey didn't seem to do much thinking, lying down or otherwise. Youngblood went in to check and saw the man motionless on his bunk; then he turned the wick away down on the lantern which hung in the corridor, and came back in to sit with Slim. "Lay down and get some sleep if you want to," he told the skinny deputy.

"Sleep!" Slim said. "Who can sleep? Listen to them rannies down town."

Youngblood leaned out on the window sill. From the White Plaza down two blocks, and more faintly from McSween's, probably also from the lobby of the Robert Lee Hotel, came loud talk and laughter and an occasional rebel yell, or what some drunken cowpoke thought was a rebel yell. The piano was clanking away down at McSween's and from the *cantina* out among the adobes the lighter tinkle of a guitar sometimes wafted across the night air.

"I'm glad we can hear them," Youngblood said. "They don't sound too serious to me. I figure we'd really be in trouble if they were quiet, many as there are in town."

"You figure they'll try anything tonight?"

"Who knows?" Youngblood said. "But if I was the sheriff I'd be doing just what he's doing. I wouldn't take any chances; if they get Ivey out of here, we'll never lay hands on him again."

"You figure we'll ever hang him?"

"I haven't given it much thought," Youngblood said. "The judge seemed to think we will."

Slim laughed. "You know what that judge puts me in mind of? A road runner I used to have; you know, a chaparral? This one had a bad leg and he would just bob along till he would get up close to me, then he would walk slow and sway just like the judge does. The craziest looking bird you ever saw, but he would stand there and look me in the eye and you could tell he didn't give a good God damn what he looked like. I believe he thought he had *me* for a pet. The only difference is that talking; that judge can sure talk."

"He makes sense," Youngblood said. He thought of something else too but didn't say it, the way a road runner will tie into a rattlesnake and peck him to death. He didn't know whether he believed that kind of comparison.

A full moon lay over the town. A hundred yards straight across the street he could see a gleam of metal coming out of a dark shadow huddled on the flat roof of the hardware store. Andy was a good man with a rifle. Young-

27

blood drew his .44 and held it out the window to see how it would sight under the moon—good enough in the short range of the street.

He still had the idea in the back of his mind about the road runner and Judge Pendergrass. He was thinking that the judge was a small man and a man of peace, not really suited to a place like Comanche Wells where every man wore a gun or kept one within reach; yet a man with a sort of bare-faced gall about him that made you wonder whether he knew something you didn't know or whether he was too innocent for his own good. He realized that this was the same way that he had sometimes thought about Lila, which proved that appearance had nothing to do with the comparison. Even though he might not be a fair judge, there was no doubt that Lila was a beautiful woman, and while the judge might not look like a road runner, he certainly was in no way beautiful. He chuckled audibly at the thought that he would kid her some day and tell her that she reminded him of a road runner.

"What the hell are you doing" Slim said, "sitting there poking your gun out the window and laughing? You must be cracking up."

"Why don't you go to sleep?" Youngblood said.

"I couldn't sleep on this bunk if they paid me," Slim said. "I sure hope I don't never do anything against the law and get put in this jail and have to sleep on one of these things."

"If I know the sheriff," Youngblood said, "along about midnight one of us is going to have to go over there and lay on top of that hard roof and relieve Andy."

It was short of midnight when they came, seven horsemen, one of them leading a riderless horse, saddled and ready. Youngblood saw them a block away, and he noticed too that the dim light which had been streaming from the sheriff's office below him had been put out at some time before. The leader of the riders was ordering them in a hoarse whisper to be quiet, but they were making noise. At Youngblood's touch Slim rose and squatted by the other window.

They stood their horses in the center of the street for

a moment, bunched behind their leader as if they had no plan. Then the leader, a hulking figure on a big paint, yelled, "Sheriff! Sheriff Bell! I know you can hear me. Listen. Nobody's going to get hurt if they act reasonable. All we want is Ivey. We're taking him out of here."

The sheriff's voice was not loud, but it carried clear in the still air. "I'm not so sure. Somebody *may* get hurt. I got a double-barrel shotgun pointed at your chest, feller. You're messing with the law." Youngblood could not see him, but he knew the sheriff must be outside, in the shadow of the building.

"Don't be a damn fool, Sheriff!" the man yelled, still loudly. "They's seven of us and no more than four of you."

"I'm not going to kill seven," the Sheriff said, "just you, Bledsoe."

"This ain't Bledsoe. And we mean business, Sheriff. "You've done your duty; now let us have Ivey, or we'll wipe you out."

"If you don't ride out of here, I'm *going* to do my duty," the sheriff threatened. "And if we kill you it's to stop a jailbreak, but if you kill anybody, it'll be murder in the first. And while you're smoking that over you might as well know we got you in a crossfire. You damn fools are setting there in the middle of the street, half drunk, and your horses are going to start bucking at the first shot; God! you don't know how close you are to dead."

"You can't bluff us, Sheriff," the man said. He was not so confident now, but obviously was not going to back down on account of words.

"Speak up, Andy," the sheriff called.

Before the words were more than out of his mouth, the rifle cracked from the roof behind them, and the white hat of the man on the end jerked forward from his head as if pulled by a string. Youngblood was thinking that it would have been better if it were the leader's, but he knew that Andy could not see the sheriff and did not want him in his line of fire. The riders were waving their revolvers, peering, hunting for targets.

Then another rifle cracked. Unbelievably it was from the other end of the courthouse. The leader's tall-crowned white hat jerked and sailed, it seemed half a block, down the street. It must have been hit in the top right in the

29

edge. The horses milled nervously, and one broke and ran back down the street. The rider was not trying hard to stop him. As the others began to follow, the bareheaded leader shook his gun in the moonlight and yelled in fury, "We'll be back, Sheriff! Damn your hide! And we'll have the crossfire! You ain't heard the last of this!"

The sheriff appeared in the street where the horsemen had been, his shotgun cradled in one arm. He studied the backs of the retreating riders and then looked up toward the second storey of the courthouse, at the end from which the second shot had come. He called, "Judge Pendergrass?"

"Yes."

"Good shot."

Youngblood leaned far out the window and added, "Nice shooting, Judge."

"Thank you, gentlemen," came the voice.

To Youngblood that one shot was more eloquent than all the talking the judge had done that afternoon. He wondered—it didn't really matter; to shoot at and hit a hat in the moonlight was a feat of markmanship—but he wondered whether the judge had aimed at the center of it and missed, or had aimed with audacity at the edge of it to make it sail.

Chapter 4

OLD MAGGIE, the cook for the jail, had brought in an uncovered tin tray with biscuits and scrambled eggs and coffee for Ivey.

Youngblood said to the sheriff, "How about me going home to get a little sleep?"

"Take that tray up to Ivey first, will you?"

Maggie said, "I'll take it up, Sheriff. That poor man likes me to wait on him." She was a heavy woman, rather sloppy in her dress, but a good cook.

"Naw, let Youngblood; I don't want you going upstairs."

"Why not? I always been feeding Mr. Ivey. That poor

man. How's he going to tell me how he likes things cooked? I been feeding him all along."

"Things changed a little bit in court yesterday," the sheriff said dryly. "Go fix me some breakfast and bring it in here."

Youngblood hung up his gun and took the tray upstairs. The prisoner was still asleep, snoring, lying with all his clothes on except his boots. "Hey, Ivey," he yelled, and kicked on the bars.

Ivey got up stretching, contemptuously ignoring Youngblood and the tray of food under the cell door. He was a man of lanky form, well-proportioned and tall. His face had the creamy pallor of one who had lived in the sun, but has been confined. His black hair and drooping black mustache showed no traces of gray; he must have been between thirty-five and fifty, but his hard face betrayed neither youth nor age. The symmetry of it was sullied by a whitish scar in the center of his forehead, a finger of which ran down through his left eyebrow. He seldom smiled, even when one would have taken his words as kidding.

He spoke only when he saw that Youngblood was turning to go. "Wait, Youngblood, you're a good guy. Tell that sheriff I've got to have a bigger cell. This thing ain't big enough for a dog. I can't get no exercise. Why don't he put me downstairs where I was?"

"I'm afraid that's it, Ivey," Youngblood said. "You'll just have to get used to it."

"Get used to it! Hell's bells! I never treated nobody this way when I was deputy. I ain't got no window where I can see what's going on, and I ain't got no decent room to do any walking. I been a deputy marshal in Oklahoma Territory and I been a sheriff in north Texas, and I sure ain't never seen a prisoner treated this way. I'd rather be chained out in the street like some dog than to be put in a little hole like this."

"I'm sorry Ivey. This is it." Youngblood turned to go.

"Wait, listen to me, dammit! That's the least you can do."

"I didn't get any sleep last night, feller. Tell it to yourself."

"Wait, Youngblood, come back here! You're worse

than the sheriff! Leave me in this little hole up here by myself! Wait! Come back here! Youngblood!"

He could hear the prisoner still shouting when he got to the bottom of the stairs. He found that Judge Pendergrass had come into the sheriff's office. The sheriff turned to Youngblood and said, "What do you think? Reckon you could get into that Cattlemen's Association meeting this afternoon? You'd have a better chance than any of the rest of us."

"Why, I don't know. I don't see why not. I can get *in*, but I don't know how long I'll stay."

"Anything we could find out would sure be worth it," the judge said. "We can't afford to wait and let them make all the moves."

"You mean for me to wear my badge and gun, don't you?"

The judge nodded.

"Sure," the sheriff said. "You got as much right there as anybody."

"Well," the judge said. "I'm not sure just where he will stand legally; it's a question of whether it's an open meeting. I wouldn't stay if the presiding officer asks you to leave. But you may pick up something. Don't fight them, Youngblood; you'll be way outnumbered. And they may be agreeable to you because you've been there before, or they may resent you strongly."

"It's at two o'clock," the sheriff said. "Go get some sleep."

When he got home, Lila wanted him to eat breakfast but he went on to the bedroom and had closed his tired eyes before his head hit the pillow.

At nine a.m. Mr. Stephen Pendergrass beat on the door of the judge's office with his balled fist. The judge opened the door, smiling, and shook hands with his brother. "Well," Stephen said, "you mean this is all there is to it? I don't have to fill out an application blank or something before I can see you?"

"No, I guess not today, Steve. Come right on in." The judge swayed back toward his desk and pushed out a wooden chair for his guest.

Looking at the brothers together, one would have seen that they were kin. They had the same steel-gray hair, the same hooked nose, the same deep-set eyes. But Stephen's face was fixed in hard dignity; his cheeks hung like the jowls of a bulldog. The judge's face was alive with his talk; behind the brass-rimmed spectacles, his eyes sparkled. Perhaps their greatest difference was in their bearing; the larger brother held his body with such pride that he could not have been the same man if he had possessed the crippled leg of the judge.

"What was wrong last night?" Stephen asked. "What have you got to do that's so important that you can't come to see your own brother?"

The judge laughed. "My job is rather demanding sometimes."

"Does it demand that you work at night?"

"Sometimes." He was determined not to apologize for refusing to come when his brother called. "Frankly, Stephen, some of your hired hands are not very tactful; they made it sound like a demand instead of an invitation, and I might not have come even if I hadn't been busy."

"Forget it," the big man said. "But I think you might come out to the house while you're in town. I hope you haven't forgotten your family just because you took on this political job. But to come to the point: I want to talk to you about William Ivey. Why did you convict him of murder and sentence him to hang?"

"Are you serious?" the judge asked.

"Of course I'm serious. I never heard of such malarky. I want to know or I wouldn't have asked you."

"Well, in the first place, Steve, there's no *malarky* about it at all. William Ivey is indeed convicted of murder and sentenced to hang. In the second place, I didn't do either one; the jury returned the verdict of "guilty" and they fixed the punishment."

"Oh, come on, Albert! God damn! Don't give me that. You can't wriggle out of it that easy. You're in charge of the court. Hell, I run the Rail-P and I'm not out there once a week, but I'll stand behind everything that's done out there. There's no question about who's running the place and who's responsible. Same way with my bank. Same way with everything I run."

The judge's face had become serious at the words "wriggle out of it." He said slowly, "It's not the same

33

way with the court I run. I run it according to proper legal procedures. I make the decisions I'm supposed to make to the best of my ability; the others I leave to those who are supposed to make them. But I do stand behind the actions of the court, Steve; I'm not trying to wriggle out of anything."

"Then why all this legal-procedures mumbo-jumbo? All this johnny-come-lately horse manure you're trying to give me? Why don't you answer my question? Why did you find William Ivey guilty and sentence him to hang?"

The judge rose and swayed his way to the open window, which looked down on the dusty main street. On two nails over the window rested the rifle he had used the night before. He was trying to think of a way to get through to his brother and at the same time keep his own temper calm.

"My johnny-come-lately procedures have been used by the English for some time," he said. "And by the Romans before that. Why do you always try to force me to defend myself, Steve? Why must you run down every position I ever hold? I'm not ashamed of my job; I'm proud of being a judge, and I'm a good one. But why should I have to defend this to you? The fact is that you are in contempt of court by your words and your attitude."

"What in the hell do you want me to do? Get down on my knees?"

The judge didn't answer.

"I invited you to my home last night," Stephen went on, "and you were busy. Now I ask you a question as a brother, and you stand on your dignity as a judge. That seems rather high and mighty to me."

"I did not think you asked me as a brother."

"Well I'm not your cousin, or a stranger. And I'm not some two-bit lawyer begging in your court. I came to ask you an honest question as a brother."

"Your question is an insult," the judge said, "but if I must, I'll answer it. Ivey was found guilty because he *is* guilty—of a heinous murder. He was sentenced to hang because that is what he deserves, and the sooner such men as he are convicted of their crimes and hanged, the sooner this country will be civilized."

Stephen Pendergrass sat in silence for a moment.

34

"Well," he said, "I finally prized an answer out of you even if it doesn't make good sense. Surely to God you must know the man's not guilty. Anybody who's got half the facts of the case can see that."

"Oh," the judge said. "How's that?"

"If he was guilty, he'd have an alibi," the big man said, almost as if it were too obvious to speak of. "You couldn't convict him if he was guilty, only if he was innocent."

"Well, that's a new one on me. Perhaps you'll explain yourself."

"I will if you'll get off of that high horse, Albert. You're not that ignorant about what's been going on. Don't you know that five rustlers have been executed in the past three years by a man acting as a vigilante, and that Ivey's been under suspicion each time, and that he's had an iron-clad alibi for each one of those killings. Yet you ask the next man you meet on the street 'who did them,' and he'll tell you 'William Ivey.' It's common knowledge. Don't you know if Ivey had killed this damned sheepherder's kid, he'd have an alibi?"

"No, I don't."

"Because you don't want to. For some self-righteous reason you mean to hang him for any crime you can."

"Steve," the judge said, "I suppose you think you're raising a serious question. Now if you want to talk to me as a brother, as you say, then use a little courtesy. I don't accept your line of reasoning. In the first place, it doesn't necessarily follow that Ivey would have an alibi. In the second place, you say a vigilante executed five rustlers! Why don't you say that five men were shot in the back? And finally, and most important, twelve men have already decided on Ivey's guilt; they knew all the rumors about Ivey that you know or I know. They searched their conscience, a jury of his peers, and found him guilty beyond any reasonable doubt."

"Searched their conscience! A jury of his peers!" Stephen mocked. "Albert, that's legalistic hogwash and it stinks! That whole jury bunch put together is not the peer of William Ivey; they're not equal to his little finger. A bunch of storekeepers and sheepherders and hayseed farmers. Everybody knew they would want to hang Ivey before they ever heard any evidence."

35

The judge chuckled. "You sound like a man who really knows what he's talking about, Steve; only you don't stick to the facts. Actually, no one thought they *would* convict Ivey, because no one thought they had the guts to bring in a verdict according to their convictions. Another little fact is that two ranchers sat on the jury."

"Ross and Chumbley! You call them ranchers? Ross may run a hundred and fifty head, and most of them he branded when they were calves running behind somebody else's cow. As for Chumbley, he's an old grandmother afraid of his own shadow."

"Steve," the judge said. His voice was calm and even gentle. "We've been talking about why I did this and why I did that. Let's talk about you. Have you really looked at this man Ivey, whom you defend? Have you considered that he is almost without doubt a paid killer, and have you considered what it means to kill other men as he has bragged of doing? And you speak of the 'damned sheepherder's kid.' Surely you have not thought about it. You have sons. Imagine a twelve-year-old boy, going about chores for his father, shot down from behind, dragging himself through the dirt; then when he is back on his feet, shot again, through the head, and his killer coming down out of his hiding place among the rocks to turn the child over with his foot. Have you really thought about this Steve?"

"I've thought about it, and not in this soft-headed way *you* think about it. I tell you Ivey didn't kill the God damned sheepherder's kid. He never killed anybody that didn't deserve killing. He killed a bunch of hostile savages when he was a scout for the army, and he was cited twice for bravery for doing it. He's done more to stop rustling than all the two-bit sheriffs and marshals in the country put together, and I think he ought to have a medal for it. Sure, I have sons, and they are soft living dudes like you seem to be now. You've lived in this country long enough to know our land is soaked with the blood of savages and greasers and rustlers."

"And twelve-year-old boys."

"But I know Ivey didn't kill the boy, dammit!"

"Someone killed the boy. I accept the jury's verdict. We are a little late, Steve, in trying this case, you and I.

36

I can see that we are not going to agree on his guilt, but for me it is already settled unless the appeal court should find an error."

The big man asked abruptly, "Why did you set a date for this hanging you think will come off?"

"You're pretty frank about what you think," the judge said, "so I will be frank. I have to start a term of court in another location on August the third. I intend to stay right here and see this matter settled legally before that date."

Mr. Steven Pendergrass rose from his chair. His appearance had changed. An explosive force seemed to lie waiting behind the harsh dignity of his face. "I've sat here wasting my time with a lot of yap, yap, yap, and you don't even try to understand me. I can't control the forces you are fighting against, and they don't know how to fight with your legalities and yap-yap. The best deputy that two-bit sheriff of yours has got is a misguided cowboy named Youngblood that used to work for Charley Moss, but I tell you there's a dozen men on every ranch in two hundred miles of here that can fight and ride and shoot as well as he can. They'll kill whoever they have to, but they won't let William Ivey hang, and I can't control them. Let me tell you something. You get out of this town, and you get back to Austin and go through whatever legal red tape you have to in order to get Ivey out of jail. Then I'll stand behind your two-bit job as a judge. Otherwise I promise nothing; I can't control the forces you're stirring up." He headed for the door.

The judge said quietly, "Please do not leave under a misapprehension, Steve. I have no intention of doing what you suggest."

"Then don't come crying to me on your knees!" the big man screamed. He seemed so carried away that he could not operate the doorknob. When he had finally opened the door, he passed through and slammed it with all his might.

The judge sat meditating. His mind went back over a half a century to the first place he could remember, their log cabin on the Navidad River. He could remember when Steve had been six, and he must have been only four. They had played together constantly. Later on they hunted together, as far west as the headwaters of the Lavaca.

37

Steve had been the same in those days, headstrong and prone to lose his temper. They had seen this land under four flags, that of Mexico, the Republic, the Union, and the Confederacy, and they had seen the blood of Indian and Mexican and settler soak into the soil. During these decades of conquest and violence Steve had fitted into it all; he had not changed except for being more successful since those days of childhood play.

As for himself, there had been two eras in his life, marked off by one summer day, hot such as this, when a half-broken mustang pony had fallen with him and crushed his leg against a rock. For twenty-eight years before that he had been able to keep up with Steve, perhaps even surpass him in agility and marksmanship if not in strength, and it had been a fine life; since that hot summer day he had not been a man at all to his older brother, had turned to books, then to the law, and might have been more than a district judge today if he had kept his mouth shut when the state argued so hotly over secession. He used to say in fun that a horse made him into a lawyer. But the second era of his life was a fine one too, because of things in his nature that were deeper than his handicap; and he felt that he would not go back to the early life even to have restored to him the strong leg he had had when he was young.

Chapter 5

YOUNGBLOOD came up to the main street and headed toward the Robert Lee Hotel, in the dining room of which the Cattlemen's Association would be already assembling for a called meeting. Ahead of him on the porch of the Alamo Groceries and Provisions Co. his attention was drawn by a Mexican man who sat on the boards and leaned back against the wall, half-hidden behind a wide-brimmed *sombrero* with pointed crown. A bench was provided beside the door, where loungers sometimes sat in the evening, but the Mexican stranger

38

sat on the floor. Youngblood noticed him because he was sure that he had seen the white flash of an eye as the *sombrero* turned down to hide the man's face. The Mexican had looked up at him but kept his head down as he approached and passed. The stranger wore clothing that was tight fitting on the legs and arms, and at his right hip a Colt revolver in a slick leather holster was tied down with thongs above his knee.

A few Mexicans worked on the ranches in the area, and a few lived in the adobe huts scattered out south of town, but a Mexican was seldom seen lounging on main street, never wearing a gun. Youngblood wondered about him; if he had been brought in by some cattleman in connection with Ivey trouble, what was he doing sitting there? It made no sense.

The block dominated by the Robert Lee Hotel was crowded with horses on either side of the street. Some few cowmen were still entering, and Youngblood was glad to see that the dining room off the lobby was already almost full. Still his badge seemed to him to stick out as a sign on a saloon. No one spoke to him as he found a chair at a table near one side of the big room.

The president of the Association was a man named Ogle, a somewhat hesitant old man with white hair, who was not a good public speaker. He tapped sporadically with a wooden mallet, standing waiting for the group to give him its attention. "I guess everybody knows why we're here," he began. "We voted a pretty big sum of money for lawyers' fees, and . . . could I have your attention, please. Anyway I understand that two of our lawyers have gone to Austin, and Mr. Pierson is here today, and I have promised . . . I have promised that we would hear him first."

Pierson, the dude lawyer who had been at the sheriff's office the evening before, was on his feet. "Gentlemen, we have a serious problem that I must bring to your attention. We have. . ."

"What kind of a meeting is this?" someone in the rear interrupted. "Ogle, the first thing we need to do is clear some of these guys out that don't belong in here."

"Yeah," someone agreed. "We need to elect us a bouncer."

39

"Hell, we don't need a bouncer. Let's just throw them out."

"There's a damned newspaper editor in here. What kind of a meeting is this supposed to be anyway?"

Editor Ezra Pitts was blushing tomato red but he said, spluttering, "I stand on my rights. I represent the free press. I demand . . ."

"They's a deputy sheriff in here, too, and a juryman, by God! that helped convict Ivey. And another feller that's been against Ivey ever since he used to work for the Association."

Youngblood thought of asking what the objections were to a deputy sheriff, whether they were planning something illegal, but he decided he might do his job of getting information better if he kept his mouth shut.

Charlie Moss rose in the confusion and answered what he had taken as an objection to him. "I been in this association ever since it started, and I got my own ideas, and I ain't leaving just because somebody don't agree with me."

Mr. Pierson was still standing and saying, "Please, gentlemen, please."

Ogle tapped some more with his mallet. "Boys, I understand . . . Uh, Mr. Pierson says we got to hear him first."

"How come?" someone asked. That was Bledsoe. Youngblood was trying to identify all the speakers that he could and remember as much as possible.

"Please, gentlemen," Pierson said. "If you will hear me, I'm sure you will agree that I should be heard first. The case is not settled yet. We have an appeal. The transcript of the trial is now on the way to Austin, and my colleagues . . ."

"Pearson, that's the same old bull you done give us once," someone said. Youngblood had seen the man before, thought he was a ramrod for Underwood's spread. "You're going to get Ivey hung," he went on. "Why should we listen to you? You've had your chance."

The dude lawyer was losing his composure. "Because! Mr. Ivey still has a legal chance, but only if you do not prejudice his appeal by some violent action. Even a rumor . . ."

While more objections and arguments were going on, Youngblood was looking over the room. About sixty men

40

were present, maybe twenty of them owners, most of the rest foremen or other hands that had extra responsibilities. He was trying to figure who it might have been leading the bunch down at the jail last night. The sheriff had thought it was Bledsoe, but it might have been any one of a half dozen. Also, maybe the unknown party who had been paying Ivey his blood money was in this room, but that was more uncertain still. He could only be certain that it *wasn't* Ogle; the man was nothing but a front; he kept looking over the room as if waiting for someone to tell him what to do. Youngblood followed his eyes but could not tell who they were questioning.

"One thing for sure, we can't talk at this meeting," a rancher named Taylor was saying. "If Mr. Pierson is finished, I would like to make a motion."

"I am finished. But I want everyone present to take notice of my warning. Even a rumor of violence can hurt . . ."

"I move that we break up this ruckus just as soon as we can figure out some place to meet where we'll have a little privacy."

"Second," someone said.

Mr. Ogle began to tap with his mallet as if he were going to call a vote.

"This association was first formed at the Rail-P," Bledsoe said. "Maybe Mr. Pendergrass would let us meet there."

Mr. Pendergrass rose on the other side of the room. Youngblood had not noticed him. The room became quiet immediately. Ogle stopped tapping.

"I would be happy to welcome some of my friends out to the Rail-P in the morning at the headquarters building," the big man said. "I believe you all know where that is. Please come at nine o'clock. Anybody that's got a long ride to make home, you're welcome to go on out to the Rail-P if you don't want to stay in town. We'll put you up some way." He was silent for a minute, turning slowly to look over the gathering. They stayed quiet. "I'm inviting just those that voted to spend Association money to defend Ivey. I think it's pretty well known how everybody voted. But this won't be an Association meeting tomorrow. If you voted against hiring

41

lawyers for Ivey, please come to see me some other time."

Youngblood was thinking about the obvious respect the crowd had for the rancher-banker and wondering whether Pendergrass would have a peacemaking effect on them. It was hard to make out the man, but he was not simply the benevolent and hospitable old man he seemed now.

The dude lawyer asked, "Do you want me out there, Mr. Pendergrass?"

The big man smiled. "Maybe the less we say here, the better. Any other invitations will be given in private." He sat down.

The men began to leave while Ogle was going through the feeble formality of adjourning. There seemed more of them when they were on their feet, and Youngblood felt a kinship with them. Most of them were in town on horseback and they were roughly dressed, a tough bunch of men, the kind that could organize a roundup and comb a thousand square miles of mountain and prairie, flushing out the half-wild cattle, bunching them, sorting, branding, marking, castrating. They were men who knew how to fight a grass fire, who knew the constant struggle to provide water, who knew what it meant to string out three thousand grown steers and point them toward Kansas. Youngblood knew their hard life, and two ideas seemed to be arguing with him in the back of his mind. The first was that the law should be with these men, not against them, for they were the backbone and sinew of the country and their business, the lifeblood of a town like Comanche Wells. The other idea concerned the fantastic odds if these men became determined to oppose the law. There were maybe no more than twenty owners present, but each of them controlled from two or three up to as many as twenty-five regular hands. The sheriff was going to need more than one or two new deputies.

He caught up with his uncle on the porch of the hotel and shook hands with him. Charlie Moss was smiling, as was his habit. He had a pink face that looked as if it had been scrubbed with a rough wash cloth. He had a reputation of being an easy man to work for. The deputy grinned. "I don't guess you'll be out at the Rail-P party tomorrow."

"I haven't got time to mess with them even if I was in-

42

vited," Charlie Moss said. "If they give me a hard time, I'm liable to hold a party of my own."

"Do you think they'll do anything, Uncle Charley?"

"They'll do something sooner or later, if those damn lawyers don't get Ivey out. They'll do something. I wish you weren't right in the middle of it, boy. Why don't you throw it over and come on out and work for me?"

Youngblood laughed and then became serious. "How did that vote go they were talking about? How many men voted to hire the lawyers for Ivey?"

"It was plenty one-sided. About ten to one. But I'm serious about you coming out to the place, son. This would be a mighty good time to quit this law job."

"That's according to how you look at it, Uncle Charlie. But I'll tell you what I would like to do. I'd like to bring Lila out there, get her out of it."

"You bring her right on, boy. She'll be welcome. Any time." Youngblood had stepped off the porch and was heading toward the courthouse when Ogle called to him, "Deputy! Say, Deputy!"

He turned and looked back, waiting.

"Could you come here a minute, Deputy?"

He went back and Ogle said, "Mr. Pendergrass asked if you would join him for a minute if you have time."

He went back into the dining room, which was almost empty now. Mr. Stephen Pendergrass was sitting alone at a table with a whisky bottle and two glasses. The big man stared at him from the time he entered the door until he stopped at the table.

"Your name's Youngblood." It was a statement rather than a question.

"Yes sir."

"Sit down, Mr. Youngblood, and join me in a drink."

"No, thank you, Mr. Pendergrass, I just have a minute."

"Suit yourself. Well, young man, I was interested in seeing you at our Cattlemen's Association meeting this afternoon. It's the first you've attended since you started working for the sheriff."

"That's right."

"Whose idea was it? Yours or somebody elses?"

Youngblood laughed. He knew that he was engaged in serious conversation, not merely passing the time of day,

43

and he wanted to find out all he could without telling anything himself. "Let's just say 'I dropped in,'" he said.

"All right, you won't tell me," the big man said. "But I'm going to be frank with you, Mr. Youngblood. If you hadn't worn that tin badge, I'd probably think you'd been trying to spy on us. As it is I think you're maybe wondering whether you're on the right side in this matter. Now, I don't think we'll have any trouble, nothing like that, but I think we may have some hard feelings, and I think before this Ivey matter is settled you, as a cattleman at heart, won't enjoy wearing that badge."

He stopped and waited. Youngblood was searching for something to say that would not sound too definite. "Well, Mr. Pendergrass, the way I look at it, I was working for the sheriff last week, and it's no time to quit now, just because things get a little tough for him."

"That's one way to look at it." The big man pulled a long cigar from his vest pocket and went through the ritual of cutting off the end and lighting it. "Another way would be to figure maybe it was time to decide where you stand. Maybe you didn't think about it last week. How much do you get paid?"

Youngblood laughed again. "I'm not sure I'm supposed to put out that information, Mr. Pendergrass. You ask the sheriff."

"Well the reason I ask, young man, I aim to be frank, as I said. I pay my hands thirty-five dollars a month. They tell me you're a top hand. I'll pay you fifty and find you a place on the Rail-P. Now, you may be inclined to say 'no' but I want you to think it over. There's another possibility; the Association has hired a detective at times in the past. You've had experience as a lawman, and if you're interested, I'll place your name before the Association; I have some influence with the other ranchers. Besides that, you may have heard that some people don't believe Bell is much of a man for the sheriff's job. He just can't handle it. I've been looking for somebody to back in the next election for sheriff. You go to work for me or the Association and do a good job, and I won't forget you. What do you say? You think it over."

"All right."

"And listen, Mr. Youngblood, this is between you and me. You think it over. You've got a right to consider a

44

better job any time you want to. If you decide to take me up, then you tell the sheriff. Until you make up your mind, it's none of his business. Right?"

"Well," Youngblood said, "I'll think it all over, Mr. Pendergrass. I better be going." The big man's eyes seemed to be piercing through him as he turned to leave.

He noticed as he came out onto the street that the Mexican gunman was gone. The man could bode no good. Youngblood made a mental note to tell the sheriff about him.

The sheriff was sitting in his office with both boots propped up on his desk. The sight struck Youngblood as funny, thinking of Pendergrass' offer, and he began laughing.

"What did you find out?" the sheriff said, lowering his feet. "And what's so damned funny?"

"I was just thinking about the offer of a job I got."

"What kind of a job?"

"A sheriff's job."

"I don't get it. Where abouts?"

"Carroll County. Mr. Pendergrass says he doesn't think you can handle the job, and he'll back me when election time comes around."

"Yeah? If you'll do what?"

"Well, that's the hitch," Youngblood said, still laughing. "I've got to quit my deputy job and go to work for him first."

"The way things look right now," the sheriff said, "I may back you myself. What did they do at the meeting?"

"The main thing they did was decide to move to the Rail-P and meet out there tomorrow, so they could be real particular about who's present. I tried to note as well as I could what . . ."

"Wait, Youngblood," the sheriff said. "Let's go up to the judge's office. I'd like him to hear everything you've got to say."

"I really haven't got much to report."

"It might not seem like much to you, or to me, but you can't tell what it might seem like to the judge." He paused, then grinned wryly. "I'd like to explain something to you, Youngblood; I don't have to explain it, but I want to. In spite of what that big-shot Pendergrass may say, I think I can handle this job."

45

"I think you can too, Sheriff," Youngblood said, chuckling but meeting his superior's eyes directly.

"I'm not running to the judge because I can't do my job. I know it's my job to keep the prisoner and to hang him if the court says hang him. But we're not playing for marbles this time. Now that damn state prosecutor ought to be giving me some help, but he's already lit out. We got to have some help in this business, and I thank my lucky stars the judge is willing. He knows the law and he knows people in Austin and he knows people here; I don't mean certain people; hell! I mean all people. Look how he told us they would try bribery, and Steve Pendergrass is already trying it on you. Youngblood, I'd rather have that little old crippled son-of-a-bitch of a judge on my side than a half-a-dozen good gun hands. Don't never sell him short. Come on, let's get up to his office."

When Youngblood had recited all that he could remember about the Cattlemen's Association meeting, he told the judge about Steven Pendergrass' offer, and the judge got a kick out of it.

"I imagine my brother is also planning to back someone else for district judge; he was rather angry with me this morning," the judge said, his eyes twinkling. "Youngblood, I believe you should string him along. Just keep on thinking it over, and if he asks you again, give some weak excuse and tell him you need more time. Anything we can fool them about will give us an advantage."

Youngblood agreed; then he told them about the Mexican stranger.

"Andy saw that Mex, too," the sheriff said. "Said he was a tough looking *hombre* with one of them long stringy mustaches they wear."

"I didn't see his face," Youngblood said, "but I'd bet money he's a gunslinger. Didn't look like a cowpoke."

"What do you think, Judge?" the sheriff asked.

"Well, it has occurred to me that some of the ranchers might bring in gunmen; they've got the money to do it if they want to. But this doesn't sound like that. What would he be doing sitting on main street?"

"Probably couldn't have anything to do with Ivey," the sheriff said. "Could he be looking over the bank?"

"I don't see how," Youngblood told him. "He was in front of the Alamo Store when I saw him."

"Well, we'll just keep our eyes open," the sheriff said.

Chapter 6

YOUNGBLOOD came back from supper to serve early guard duty at the jail. He went upstairs to get Ivey's supper tray and see that everything was all right. The prisoner was lying with his bare feet propped against the bars, fussing as usual. "Youngblood, I'll swear to God, I didn't think you all would treat a white man this way. When are you going to let me out there in the hall where I can get a little exercise?"

"August the first," Youngblood said.

"Youngblood, you sure are a funny man. I wish you was laying in here and could see yourself out there."

"If I was in there," the deputy said, "I would probably be praying instead of raising cane."

"You probably would, Youngblood. You're real funny that way. This whole damned town is funny. Comanche Wells! You know something? There never was a stinking Comanche that had a well. They take their water where they find it, and if they don't find any they go without. It was the God damned *padres* that built the well. But you know something? It wasn't even a well in the first place; it was a seep, just a seep with some rocks stacked up around it. And if that ain't funny enough for you, the thing wasn't here; it was three miles up Seedy Creek, up in the brakes. Now, where does that put your town?"

Youngblood could not see the expression on his face, only the scar on his forehead and his eyes shining in the lantern light. "How do you know so much about it?" the deputy asked.

"Hell, boy, I been through this country long before this funny town was built. I was tried and sentenced to die right about here twenty years ago, by a bunch of damned savages that knew how to try a man so's it would scare the living daylights out of him. They left this half-breed buddy of mine with an arrow through him and his scalp lifted and him still alive, laying out on the prairie, just laying there with his bloody head in the dirt. And they brought me down to the creek and tied me to a cotton-wood tree. Well, the whole blooming night they argued over me. They was one big buck that thought he was the leader; he wanted to target practice on me with their arrows and lances; they didn't have any guns. Then they was a younger buck that was a chief's boy; he wanted to stake me out naked in the sun or else drag me behind their ponies. They argued the whole blessed night. When morning come, they sighted a herd of buffalo and that busted up the trial; they all mounted up and took off after the buffalo, and left me tied to that cottonwood. Well, it got hot along in the morning and I begin to sweat on that rawhide and spit on it and finally slipped loose."

Ivey laughed, not as if something were funny, but as if the laugh were part of the story. "They're a real ugly bunch, Kiowas, and they look worse to a man tied up like that and knowing what they're arguing about. But I got out of there, Youngblood, and you know how many Kiowas has paid me back for that night? Plenty. After going through that Kiowa trial I figure this white-man trial is kind of a joke. I got me a ace in the hole, and I'm going to get out of here like I done before. Only thing that ain't funny about it is what I aim to do to every-body that don't treat me right."

"Is that supposed to be a threat?" Youngblood asked.

"You God damned right it's a threat, Deputy!"

He could feel the prisoner's fierce insistence, his violent will, as if it were a thing that projected through the bars. "You're not in a very good place to be making threats, Ivey," he said. "Why don't you calm down and stop riding yourself so hard?"

"Why don't you all treat me like a man and give me some room to walk around? The sheriff put me in this little hole where I can't even see outside just to spite me. You could take me out of here right now and take me for a walk if you wanted to treat me decent; you could hold a gun on me."

"Maybe I could, but I won't."

48

"You're scared. You could hold a gun on me."

"I just about halfway believe I could keep you prisoner without a gun," Youngblood told him. "But we won't ever find out, because we're not going to try it. Why don't you stop this bitching and not take it so hard? You want me to bring you something to read?" He started to leave, wishing that he had never stopped to listen in the first place.

"Read! No, wait, Youngblood! Don't go off. At least stay here and talk to me. Wait a minute. Youngblood!"

As he walked home in the middle of the night he tried to think what his argument would be to Lila. He had already mentioned that he wanted to take her out to the ranch, but it wasn't settled. A lamp was burning in the front room, and she met him at the door as he had known she would.

"Look here, young lady," he said, "do you know what time it is?"

"Well, I thought it was about time you came home to your wife."

"It's past midnight. And what are you doing? Sitting here waiting for me when you should have been in bed four hours ago. Then you come running to the door like some little feist."

She laughed and snuggled against him.

"You've been cooking and working out in that garden all day," he went on, "and then you sit up till midnight by yourself, wondering when I'll be home."

"But I wasn't alone all the time," she said. "Mrs. Ainslee was here, and she sat with me and we gossiped till after ten."

"Well, that's worse, Lila. That woman talks too much. I'm going to get you out of all this. I talked to Uncle Charley about it today, and they'll be tickled to have you."

"Let's talk about it tomorrow."

"I want you to get ready to leave tomorrow," he said, not wanting to leave it unsettled any longer. "I'll take you the first time I can get a half day off. I've got a job to do, honey, nights, days, whenever I'm needed, as long as I'm needed. The sheriff's going to start wanting me to sleep at the jail; he just doesn't have enough

49

help. I can't have you waiting up and wondering what's the matter if I don't come home right at a certain time. And I want you to be somewhere where you won't hear all this crazy gossip, and where they'll take care of you. And besides it's cooler out there."

"Will it really be better?" Her question was the simplest he could imagine, as if she were a child and he were a man who knew everything there is to know.

He nodded.

"All right," she said. He knew it wasn't all right with her but she accepted his belief that it would be better, and it was a kind of admission from her that it had been harder than she had been willing to say. She would pack tomorrow and buy a few things and get that knitting pattern for the baby bootees.

Before the time of Lila, in Bart Youngblood's life were many good memories and bad memories, solid things out of his youth, and one great passion that was more dream than reality. Among the fine solid things were his mother, his uncle, his aunt; the passion was his father, a gay adventurer who had led his young wife and baby boy along a rough road in Kansas, Oklahoma, and Texas during the troubled times before the war. The boy never had a chance to judge his father; he came to the age when a boy worships his father, and he did worship thoroughly. Then there was one final image: a big man, strong, competent, brave, jovial, in a new gray uniform, completely wonderful, going away with Hood's Brigade, going with other wild and careless men—a man who must have seen himself somewhat as the boy saw him and certainly did not suspect that of every nine who went with Hood, only one would come home.

Word came that his father lay badly wounded in a hospital. His mother, feeling that she must go, left him with her brother, Charlie Moss, and went to the place where her husband died of gangrene and she died of influenza and malnutrition.

Charlie Moss was disgusted at the rankling hatred and the carpetbaggers. He sold out and headed farther west, taking with him his wife, Annie, his two daughters, and the orphaned boy. In the boy's mind, the image never faded.

50

Life on the ranch was another of the fine solid things. At fifteen, after much begging and many objections from his Aunt Annie, he persuaded his Uncle Charlie to let him live in the bunkhouse with the three regular hands. He took part in their work and their horseplay, their wrestling, their bare-knuckle fighting which they did for the sheer joy of it. He took part in the throwing of knives at the toes of each other's boots as they sat in the bunkhouse, a game Charlie Moss made them stop when they began to use pistols. At eighteen, after he had finished all the schooling available, he began to draw the pay of a regular cowhand.

In his mid-twenties, he had behind him three long trips to Dodge City and he could work as a top hand on anybody's spread. He had grown up thinking that rough physical activity is fun. The image of his father did not crumble, but stayed a never-mentioned dream with a moral he only faintly understood—what you treasure most is not real but a vision to bring out for company on a lonely ride; and if you come to worship something real, it will die. His rough and active life was purposeless.

Then in one short minute, standing in front of a saloon in Comanche Wells, he faced the second passion of his life. A girl came out of the drygoods store and walked down the street. He spilled the cigarette he was making. His buddy laughed at him and said, "She ain't for the likes of you, cowboy."

Her name was Lila Lavinia Benson, and he had never seen anyone like her. She was not like the dance hall floozies, nor the hard-faced women on the ranches, nor even his two cousins who had giggled a lot when they were younger and as they became older were full of petty intrigues. Furthermore, she had the unlikely position of schoolteacher, when anyone knew the schoolteacher was supposed to be able to whip the biggest boy in school.

He courted her without admitting to himself what he was doing, for he felt certain that he had no chance and told himself that he only wanted to be around where she was. The first thing he did was name his long-legged mare "Lila," and after the spring roundup was over, he rode her in the big race which finished at a line across main street made by a bootheel dragged in the dirt at

51

about the place where the new courthouse was being planned. It was the first race the mare ever lost, for coming up the stretch between the straggling crowd of spectators on either side he had found himself unwilling to apply the quirt and was beaten by a horse that the mare could run circles around.

The second high point in his courtship was a failure also. After they were speaking acquaintances, he had made her an offer; if any of the big boys in school ever made trouble, let him know and he would sure take care of it. She laughed at him. How he envied the snotty-nose kids and the gangling boys who sat all day in the schoolroom with her.

He had not worked for Charlie Moss for a couple of years but had worked at miscellaneous ranch jobs between cattle drives. He came to spend too much time in town and lost his job on a fencing crew. This was about the same time that he had the audacity to ask her to go to a square dance with him. That she accepted and seemed to enjoy herself was such a surprise that he let the cattle drive leave without him. He applied for a job as deputy sheriff. Being known as a tough young man and one of the rare ones who had finished school, he got the job. To live in the same town with her was a fine thing, but he thought that she must be dedicated to a life of teaching or else would marry the middle-aged bachelor school principal or maybe a young merchant with slicked-down hair and good prospects. He had no idea that he was the leading contender.

There was a night when he rode alone for hours under the moon, battling with himself, visiting the vision of his father, trying to reckon the girl. His love for her had messed him up as a cowhand and would probably mess him up as a lawman. He determined to have it over with, to ask her the ridiculous question. What would come afterward was vague; he would never forget her, but he would have to leave and never see her again. Maybe he would try to get on a drive to Montana and stay up there.

She said, "Yes." It was that damn simple. She cried a little and laughed at him and said, "I wondered if you would ever ask me."

52

Lila was packed and resigned to going out to the Moss ranch, the Circle-2, for her month of confinement, but Youngblood found he couldn't get off the next day.

The sheriff already had a trip planned for him, out twelve miles east to the little spread of Earnest Long, who had worn the sheriff's badge before Bell.

Now the sheriff thought there might be a chance to bring Long back to wear a deputy's badge for a month. "Don't rile him up or anything, now," the sheriff said. "Just tell him I'd sure appreciate it if he'd come in to see me. What I really want is to get the judge to talk to him. He won't come for the money, but the judge might talk him into it. Besides that, he owes me a favor; I went to work for him when he was short handed. But don't say anything about the favor, Youngblood; just tell him I'd sure appreciate it if he could get in to talk to me."

He caught up the big bay gelding, which was his favorite among the sheriff's string, and set out in the middle of the afternoon, east along the stagecoach road, thinking to get to Long's place after most of the day's work was done. The bay had a smooth fox trot that ate up the miles.

The telegraph line beside the road seemed to add to the loneliness of the empty spaces. The skinny pine poles were strangers to this dry land, tied together by a sway-back line of wire, the same pattern of rising wire and crossed pole and falling wire receding into the far distance, smaller and smaller, disappearing into the heat waves, then reappearing like a toy as it went over a rise. The dusty, unkept road curved around and fitted itself to the land, but the telegraph line was perfectly and unnaturally straight, like a measure of the distances back east to civilization.

He mulled over the fact that the sheriff had sent him, and not Andy or Slim. It was important enough that the sheriff himself would have made the trip if he hadn't felt obliged to stay in Comanche Wells. It was plain that he, Youngblood, was becoming something like a chief deputy. He knew it was because the ranchers were supposed to be more sympathetic toward him, but it was a source of pride, too. It was good to know that he was doing a good job and that the sheriff trusted him. Along with the relief he would feel when he quit the job a few

53

weeks from now would be the wish that things were different, so he could stay on. Maybe in a few years when things were running smoother, he would talk it over with Lila and decide to try a lawman's job again. But, hell, that's what a lawman's job is; making things run smooth when they're rough; it would always be that way.

Maybe there was even more to it than that. Maybe if a man wants a home and children he has to be ready to do what they were asking Long to do now, come back and stand up for the law when things are rough.

He came up to the sorry little ranch house an hour before sundown. He saw a couple of men down about the barn but tied his horse and knocked at the house. The pinch-faced woman who opened the door a crack stared at him with unwelcome written on her face.

"Yes?"

He tipped his hat. "I'm looking for Mr. Long, m'am. Mr. Earnest Long."

"He don't want to see you."

"Well, if I could just speak to him a few minutes, m'am. I've ridden clear from town."

"You're wasting your time, mister star-toter. But if you're dead set on seeing him, he might be around the barn or lot someplace."

He led the big bay down and tied him at the horse trough, and ex-sheriff Long came out of the barn to meet him. The man had a weathered and hard-bitten look about him, but he did not seem as unfriendly as the woman had. They shook hands and passed pleasantries about the condition of the range and the water supply.

"I guess you know I didn't just come out here to visit, Mr. Long," Youngblood said. "Sheriff Bell sent me. He would sure be obliged if you could get in to talk to him sometime in the next few days."

"What about?"

"Well, I'd rather he'd tell you."

"I can't come on that, Youngblood. I'm working seven days a week. I got fences to fix and a tank to clean out before the fall rains. I'll have a man in town for provisions in the next few days, but I don't aim to be in myself for a month." He spoke as if he already had guessed what the sheriff wanted and as if it were already settled in his mind.

54

"Well, I don't reckon it's any big secret, Mr. Long," Youngblood said. "It's this Ivey trouble; the sheriff needs every kind of help he can get. He said he'd be mighty obliged if he could just talk to you. I know he's always spoken highly of you as a law officer."

"He don't want to talk to me about Ivey," the old man said. "I'm neutral, see. Neutral!" He swept his arms in a gesture that seemed to include the whole country. "It's the biggest mess I ever saw, and I got no part in it. It's been brewing a long time. If juries and judges and everybody concerned had done what they should about rustling around here ten years ago, you wouldn't never had Ivey here in the first place. There's no right and no wrong in the whole mess, and I don't want no part in it."

"But, sir, don't you think in a mess like this there's a time when you can draw a line and take a stand. I don't mean to tell *you* what's right and what's wrong, but I know you were sheriff in this county from the time it was first organized, and you know what it means to uphold the law. Ivey has committed a crime nobody can excuse; he's been legally convicted. Now the question is if the sentence is going to be carried out or not."

"No, it's not that simple, Youngblood. Listen to me a minute; this country is going to have law that can stand up when the people are ready for it, and not before. And I'm not going to be one of the lawmen that tries to wet nurse them into it. You can get four lawmen killed in this mess and not rush up the progress of law four years. We'll have law when we get ready for it."

The man's last statement caused Youngblood to see red for a moment. He wanted to yell, I'm ready for it *now*; I've got a wife and I hope to have a child, and this place is my home, and I want a decent place to live.

Long turned and shouted some orders to a man who was feeding a team of mules in one of the stock pens. Youngblood could see a couple of riders coming from toward town, loping their horses, stringing a cloud of dust behind them. Long did not seem surprised to see them. The deputy decided to try one more argument; the sheriff surely couldn't object to his mentioning it now. "I got the idea, Mr. Long," he said, "that maybe you owed Sheriff Bell a favor."

"Maybe I do and maybe I don't," the old man said. He

55

was getting angry. "Listen here, young man! I've got to get along with the other cowmen around here. I've still got some cows on the free range and I've got fence in common with other owners, and there's a hundred ways I got to get along with them."

"But, sir, this isn't a fight between the law and the cattlemen."

"That's what they're making it, and I got to get along with them." The old man didn't seem to like his own argument. "Besides, I told my wife I'd stay out of it." He obviously didn't like this argument either. "Listen, young man, Bell says I owe him a favor. I know what he wants; he wants me to come back and put on a badge. That ain't no favor; that's suicide. The answer is 'no.'"

The two riders reined up at the horse trough, their horses lathered all along the sides and neck. "Don't let them horses drink and them hot as they are!" Long said.

They dismounted and one, a heavy hulk of a man, said, "They wanted to know where abouts you were, Mr. Long. What's this damned two-bit deputy doing out here?"

Youngblood stared at the man, trying to place him. Not from away back, but from the last few days.

Long said, ignoring the question, "You boys rub down them horses, then turn them out. Burge, you know better than to run a horse that way when there ain't no need."

So the big man's name was Burge. The name didn't mean anything. It was the way he had sat his horse there for a moment before dismounting that looked familiar. And the voice.

"What are you doing away out here in the open by yourself, star-toter?" Burge said. "I heard you and them other cowards in the sheriff's office like to hole up and take pot shots at people."

Two ideas struck Youngblood at the same time; this was the day of the big meeting at the Rail-P, and that's where they had been. And this feller, Burge, had been the leader of the bunch that had demanded Ivey's release that first night after the conviction. Along with these ideas came a tingling around his back and neck he had felt before when a fight was brewing. He did not answer the man.

"What's the matter, star-toter? Besides being a traitor,

56

you're yeller too. How would you like me to mop up this ground with them fancy duds of yours?"

Youngblood was measuring the man, thinking that he was strong as a yearling bull, but maybe a little heavy to be very fast. He was also thinking that in the weeks ahead it would be nice for hotheads like this man to know that the lawmen of Carroll County were not push-overs but would fight, really fight. And something else was welling up in the deputy that had nothing to do with thinking; it came out of the tension of the last few days and out of Long's devious refusal, and it was surging up into savage rancor. When he spoke to Long and the other cowpoke he was surprised to hear his voice, quiet, almost calm. "Are you two fellers going to stay out of this?"

"I'm neutral," Long said. "I don't want no part of it." He had forgotten his orders about the horses. The other cowpoke sidled over beside Long to indicate his "neutrality."

Youngblood took off his gunbelt and carefully leaned it with his hat and badge against the bottom of the wooden horse trough. There was no decent way to avoid the fight at all and he was glad of it. He had scuf-fled with men as big as Burge from the time he had been sixteen years old; now he meant to make his mark. He said nothing, but inside he was screaming taunts, shaming Long—it's suicide to work for the sheriff! We're weak sissies! A crippled judge, a lonesome sheriff, and three maverick kids for deputies! He was more angry with Long than with the big-featured man he was about to fight.

"I'm going to teach me a deputy sheriff not to go out in the country by hisself!" Burge bragged, starting his rush before he got the words out and before the deputy had straightened up.

Youngblood slid backward and caught him with a solid right into the side, then straightened himself on the balls of his feet. Burge turned and came again, slower, more warily. Youngblood feinted with his left toward the head, then slammed the right home again, at the same spot in the rib cage. It felt plenty solid; he might have got a rib, and he hadn't been touched yet.

Burge bellowed something unintelligible and came

in with his arms high, like a bear, taking all he had to take to close with the deputy. Youngblood landed two glancing blows before he backed into the rump of a spooking saddle horse, and trying to avoid a possible flying hoof, tumbled backward into the dirt. He was rolling when Burge came down on him. The man was sure enough as strong as a yearling bull and almost as heavy. The deputy was halfway pinned, and took a big knee in his own belly before he screwed around enough to roll and find his feet again. He knew by then that it might cost him his life to be pinned on the ground by the heavy man.

Burge came at him again, fists flying. Youngblood ducked and dodged, but found it almost impossible to block the powerful man's blows. He took one in the left eye that caused him to see flashing lights and a glancing blow on the cheek; it stung and he knew that he had lost some skin. But it was the kind of fight he wanted. He danced in and out, and once again, coming out of a low crouch, he dug the right into the side. Burge dropped his left arm to cover the tender place, his face wincing with pain, and rushed in again to close. Youngblood uncorked the right again. It struck the big man in the throat, under the chin; he reeled backward off his feet.

When Burge came up his eyes were glassy. He was halfway out. Youngblood felt no pity about it. The tension he had felt when he knew they were going to fight had not abated; it had built up with the blows he had taken himself. He was not screaming sarcastic taunts inside now, but crying, This country is my home, and I want a decent place to live.

The big hulk of a man might have quit had there been no witnesses, but he came in, still grasping, having forgotten about his side. Youngblood stepped in to meet him this time and hit him in the same place under the left arm. Burge groaned as if the words were vomit, "God! you've busted me in!" and stumbled against the horse trough. Then he slowly slid down into the mud, unconscious.

As Youngblood buckled on his gun, he saw his arms and hands trembling like leaves of grass in gusty wind. The old man was saying, "Deputy, get on your horse and

58

get out of here," and to the other cowpoke, "Get some water on him. Use your hat. Stretch him out and get some water on him."

The sun was down. He had ridden half an hour toward town before he could think calmly. Then he chuckled to himself. As he caressed the skinned cheek and the eye that would be a beautiful blue tomorrow, he thought that he would have to tell the sheriff the truth, but he might make Lila believe his horse had thrown him into a mesquite bush.

Chapter 7

THE SHERIFF was talking with Youngblood about the Mexican gunman who had been in town three days now without anybody finding out where he came from or what his purpose was. The sheriff had decided it was time to find out something but doubted that they would get anywhere with questions. But even as they sat there considering the matter, a knock came at the open door of the sheriff's office, and they looked up to see the subject of their conversation standing before them.

He had his wide-brimmed hat in his hand. The brown skin of his hawk-like face was wrinkled, but his hair, which was plastered down, and his long thin mustache were pure black, with no gray. His dark eyes darted about constantly, searching. He wore no gun.

"Might I see Senor Ivey?" he asked the sheriff. He seemed to be in no uncertainty about whom to ask.

"Who are you?" the sheriff asked.

"Torres."

"Well, are you a lawyer or something? What do you want to see him about?"

"No, Senor Sheriff. I am just his friend."

"Well, I don't know, Mr. Torres. What do you want to see Ivey about?"

"One wants to see his friend. Perhaps I would want to tell him goodby."

"How long have you known Ivey?"

59

"Some years, Senor Sheriff."

Youngblood thought he could tell that the sheriff was about to say "no." The Mexican's answers were as simple and straightforward as they could be, but they told nothing. The sheriff studied the man for a minute. The eyes of Torres flicked about the room, taking it all in.

"Mr. Torres," the sheriff said finally, "you can see Ivey, but not right now. Come back in an hour; come back at three o'clock."

The Mexican bowed without a word and left.

"I may have me an idea, Youngblood," the sheriff said. "Go get Slim. I think he's out at the corral."

Youngblood brought the other deputy into the office. The sheriff evidently had some kind of a plan that pleased him. He asked Slim, "How good can you speak Spanish, Slim?"

"Oh, not real good. Good enough to get by, I guess. I know all the cuss words. Ching-gow! Cathrones! Borreguerro!"

"All right. All right," the sheriff said. "What I want to know is if two fellers are talking Spanish can you tell what they say even if they talk fast?"

"Sure, I can tell."

"All right. I've told that damned Mex he can see Ivey. I'm pretty sure Ivey can talk Spanish, and I bet my bottom dollar that's what they'll do. I want you to take him up there, and if they start talking Spanish, you just stand there like you don't give a hoot. You just let them rip. No matter what they say, don't give a sign you understand; just let them talk all they want to. Be sure and don't say any Spanish words yourself. You just stand there and whistle a little and clean your fingernails—they need cleaning anyway."

"Hell, I been out cleaning the horse stalls. You expect my fingernails to be clean?"

The sheriff chuckled. "No, I don't guess so. You get the idea, Slim?"

"Sure. I'll call him Mr. Torey. I don't know nothing about Spanish."

When the Mexican presented himself at three o'clock, the sheriff put on a good act. He had opened the wooden filing cabinet and spread on his desk a mess of papers. "Well, me and Deputy Youngblood are still tied up with

60

all this paperwork," he told the man. "Slim, I wonder if you would show Mr. Torres up to see Mr. Ivey?"

"Sure, where is Mr. Ivey? Upstairs?"

"Yes. In one of the back cells."

"Right this way, Mr. Torey," Slim said.

They bent over the papers until the Mexican was out of the room; then the sheriff began pacing up and down. "I hope we get something out of this," he said.

"What are you thinking?" Youngblood asked. "That this Torres may be hired by the same feller that had Ivey hired?"

"It could be. Or he could be hired by the whole bunch of cattlemen. I figure they'd rather take Ivey out by some trick than by force. We can look for some trick."

"But Sheriff, I saw this Mex before the Cattlemen's Association meeting that day, and they were real disorganized. A lot of them were thinking along the same lines, but you could tell they hadn't got together on it. I don't believe the Association itself had done anything then such as bring in a man from the outside."

"It don't make sense," the sheriff said. "But maybe we'll . . ."

A commotion of some kind had started upstairs. Slim's voice came muffled, then broke out loudly. "Shut up! Cut it out! Dammit, shut up!" There was the shuffling of boots in a scuffle. "Sheriff! Sheriff! Youngblood! Shut up! Damn you greasy bastard! Cut it out! Get out of here! Sheriff!"

Youngblood beat the sheriff to the hall door and the stairs by two strides and ran up three steps at a time. He was almost knocked down by the Mexican, who was being hazed along the upstairs corridor by Slim. The Mexican was making some sign to Ivey, who was standing, clutching the bars in his cell. Slim knocked down the Mexican's upraised hand.

"What in the Sam Hill's going on here?" the sheriff bellowed.

"That's what I'd like to know," Slim said, still hazing the Mexican away, down the stairs. "I sure can't make no Spanish out of it. Of all the grunting and waving hands I ever saw!"

Once the Mexican was away from Ivey, he went under his own power, down the stairs, into the office, and straight on into the street.

"Wait a minute," the sheriff said. "What's going on here, Slim? How come you didn't do like I told you?"

Slim shook his head. "I sure tried to, Sheriff. I kept standing there whistling and cleaning my fingernails like you said and trying to make it out."

"Couldn't you hear them?"

"Sure I could hear them. And see them! They just grunted and moved their fingers this way and that, and I could tell they were talking, but I damned sure couldn't make Spanish out of it."

"Didn't you get *anything*? Not a word at all? I thought you could speak Spanish."

"I got one word. The Mex called Ivey 'Beel.' "

"Beel? Goodnight, Slim! I sure thought you could speak Spanish. Now there's no telling what they told each other."

Later that afternoon Judge Pendergrass affirmed what was in the back of Youngblood's mind. "Did they make a sign like this?" the little judge asked, cupping his hands. "Or this?" Drawing both hands toward his chest.

"Yeah!" Slim said. "They did that. That last. The Mex did that!"

"What is it, Judge?" the sheriff asked. "Make some more signs. What kind of talk is it?"

The judge shook his head. "I don't know enough about it to figure out anything they said. A lot of Indians mix up their talk with signs, especially if they're not from the same tribe. Karankawa, Tonkawa, Lipan-Apache, Comanche, Kiowa. Who knows?"

"You think we ought to arrest him, Judge?"

The judge chuckled. "Well, it's not against the law to speak an Indian tongue. You might hold him a couple of days if you want to. He sure would bear watching. He doesn't fit in."

It was Friday, the seventh of July, before Youngblood could get the time off to take Lila out to the Circle-2. They set out in a livery-stable buggy early in the morning; he figured it would take four hours. They should get there before it got real hot. The road south along Seedy Creek was rough, and he let the mare pick her way, so that it would be easy riding for Lila; then as they

62

turned away from the creek out into the flats, he urged the mare into a trot.

They spoke little but a world of unspoken feelings rode with them on the buggy seat, for they had not been apart since their marriage.

"Where will you eat?" she asked.

"At the jail. Maggie cooks big all the time. That's one way I'll get even with the sheriff for working me so hard; I'll eat and sleep on him."

"She seems like a nasty old woman to me." A light kidding jealousy was in her voice.

"Aw, Maggie's all right. She's clean with her cooking."

"If you get tired of what she fixes, you go down to the hotel," Lila said. "I want you to eat three meals a day."

"All right."

"You promise?"

"I promise."

"You'll go out to our house some, won't you? And make sure everything is all right? I wish you would water my cantaloupe vines; the ones in the shade are still blooming, and they might make some more melons."

"All right," he said, "but you know what?"

"What?"

"We may not ever live there again. I hope to go to work for Uncle Charlie within a month from now. I want you to look at a place out here maybe a quarter of a mile the other side of the ranch house. There used to be a cabin and there are still two big pecan trees. We might build us a house there; I know Uncle Charlie wouldn't mind."

"And we would sell our house in town?"

"I reckon."

"It's kind of sad, isn't it?" she said. "I mean it seems like it's our home, and we're been proud of it."

"Yeah."

It was a pleasure for him to come into the Circle-2 headquarters; to him the sprawling ranch house meant friendliness, hard work, good food, for Lila he knew it would come to mean security and peace. He knew the place like the back of his own hand, and on this hot July day it might have been symbolized in his mind by the deep cistern on the screened-in porch, where the water came up cool on the hottest day. His uncle had come out the front door before he had stopped the buggy, and Aunt Annie came following him to welcome them, her ample bosom and hair knot jiggling to her movements.

He agreed to stay for dinner, the noon meal, and he saw during the next two hours his aunt take Lila under her wing like a big motherly Rhode Island Red with one chick. Poppies and cannas were fighting the hot air to bloom in the yard, and in the house big flowers adorned the wall paper; this was Aunt Annie's doing, but it might have been Lila's. He thought everything was going to be all right.

After dinner, she took him in to see her room. It was light and fairly cool. She kept her face turned from him as they talked lightly about it. Then he said, "Well, Lila, I've got to get going. I've stayed longer than I should."

When she turned, he saw that tears were running down her cheeks in streams. Her face was not twisted, and her lips were not trembling, but the tears came out one after the other and followed down the wet paths on her face. She stood looking at him and did nothing to wipe them away.

"Don't do that, baby," he said. "It won't be long."

"I'm not doing anything," she said. "I'm not crying. It's just . . . You know how silly pregnant women are."

She had that barefaced look, young, helpless, tears welling out of her eyes, and she stood there straight and unashamed, not smiling and not frowning, looking at him as if she would never see him again. The vision of her face and the simplicity and the tears fixed itself into his mind; he was to see it in memory again and again during the lonely days ahead. He kissed her and left without saying anything more.

His uncle helped him put the mare to the buggy again. He was on the seat and on the point of leaving, when he impulsively asked the older man. "Uncle Charlie, I don't plan on stopping any lead, but what if I did? What if I get killed next week?"

His uncle put his foot up on the hub of the buggy wheel and grinned. "I don't figure you will either, boy, but I'm glad you asked me. It don't hurt a man to know where he stands. If you was to get killed, she would be just like a daughter to me and Annie."

"And the child?"

"It would be just like a grandbaby to me and Annie, boy."

"She's got folks in Denver, but I don't think she'd want to go to them" He laughed. "I'm just talking, Uncle Charlie. I don't plan to stop any lead. You'll see me out here looking for a job inside of a month."

"The sheriff don't mean to back down an inch, does he?"

"Nope, he sure doesn't, Uncle Charlie."

"I wish you were out of it. But you can't hardly quit now. Well, be careful, boy."

He left the Circle-2 toward Comanche Wells by the same road that he had come by, but two miles out he veered west into the alkali country known as Wild Dog Flats. The land was as smooth and lonely as still water. It's barren stretches were broken only by scattered bunch grass and sometimes stingy clumps of yucca. Far across it to the southwest he could see through the waves of heat where the foothills broke out abruptly in red clay banks; farther still, across a hundred miles of hills, the purple granite of the Sierra Guadarrama lay like a cloud on the horizon.

He was heading for the rough country where Wild Dog Flats was broken by the creek as it came out of the hills. It was out of his way a little, and he didn't know for sure why he was taking such a route. He knew what was there; he had thought about it in silence while driving out with Lila. But he didn't know what he was looking for.

Neither the flats nor the foothills in this area would support cattle. It was here that the sheepman Munson had brought what the cowmen called his "stinking woolies" when he was driven out of the other free range to the north, and it was here that the sheriff had come in early spring in answer to the frantic appeals of a young Mexican herder to investigate the murder of a twelve-year-old boy. Munson's spread stretched through this desert wherever there was scattered grass or foliage of any kind. Youngblood had never seen his home.

He was trying to straighten out in his mind the events concerned with the Ivey trouble. He already knew what he was going to do; you don't quit a job because it gets tough. But words about loyalty and words about law

65

didn't argue strongly enough with the wordless tears of Lila's. Out here at Munson's might be another piece of argument.

He saw sheep sign. The dirt was cut by their small hooves as if harrowed; their hard droppings littered the ground. He saw the sheep before he saw the house. They were bunched, two acres of them, on a gravel bar on the inside of a bend of the creek, like light-gray froth cast up out of the water hole there. Then he saw the house, under an outcrop of rock on this side of the creek. It was by all odds the sorriest house he had ever seen. It was made of skinny whitened driftwood limbs, larger ones at the four corners, smaller ones for the walls, standing side by side as nearly upright as crooked limbs can stand; a similar mess made up the roof. The cracks were stopped with daubings of mud, much of which had fallen off and lay on the ground around it. The door and one window were covered with burlap.

He stopped the buggy and hailed, "Hello! Hello, in there!" Down two-hundred yards nearer the creek a movement caught his eye, and he saw the figure of Munson. He was working with a long handled shovel.

Youngblood drove down, tied the lines to the whip handle, and walked up to the man. Munson was scraping with the shovel, drawing the red earth up into two mounds. He did not offer to shake hands but said, "Coyotes. They keep trying to dig in. Have to get me some rocks and put over them."

Youngblood did not understand. It looked like two graves the man had mounded up. Munson was dressed in dirty trousers and straw hat. He wore no shirt. His arms and chest were burned dark red. His beard was matted around his slack mouth. He kept one eye on the herd of sheep down by the bend as he scraped at the clods of clay.

"I was going back into Comanche Wells, Mr. Munson," Youngblood said. "I thought I'd stop by. I thought you might have a letter to mail or something."

"I don't write no letters," the sheepman said. He pounded at one of the mounds with the shovel and looked at the sheep. A collie dog was padding his careful way along the outskirts of the herd.

66

"Is this where you buried your boy?" the deputy asked.

The man nodded. "And my old lady. He killed her too, my old lady."

"What? What do you mean, Mr. Munson?"

"Sure. This one's her. That one there's the boy."

"But I don't understand. Is your wife dead? She was all right when the sheriff was out here."

"Sure, she's dead. Goddam his stinking soul to hell! He killed my old lady sure as he killed my boy."

"What do you mean, Mr. Munson? When did your wife die?"

"Four-five days ago. She didn't have nothing. I had my sheep and my dog; all she had was the boy. She didn't like this place anyway; didn't like the house, neither. When that son-of-a-bitch killed my boy, she taken it into her head to die on purpose. Wouldn't cook; wouldn't eat what I cooked. Wouldn't come out of the house. Wouldn't go back in the house." The man's eyes were on his sheep. He put two fingers to his slack mouth and drew it tight and whistled so shrilly that the sound could hardly be heard. The collie sprang up and went after a dozen sheep that were straggling down the creek bank.

"Used to pick flowers," the man went on. "In the early spring she would take the boy way up the creek and they would tote home flowers to clutter up the house. And the boy would pick them when he was watching sheep—bring them to her. That's all she done, my old lady, after that son-of-a-a bitch killed the boy—pick Indian Paint Brushes and bring them down here. That's all was growing that late in the year, Indian Paint Brushes, and she piled them up on his grave." He cut at the dried stems with the shovel blade.

Youngblood could see that the dried stems had been flowers. There had been a lot of them. It was a barren place for burying people, no grass and no trees, but the smaller grave had once been piled high with desert flowers.

"Goddamn his filthy stinking soul to hell!" the sheepman said. "I'll tell you something, Deputy, I never told at the trial. He came through here and I cussed him, but did that give him any leave to come back and kill my boy? He come riding through highhanded and scattered

67

my sheep over forty acres, and I admit I cussed him. I never said anything about the cussing, because I want the filthy, low-life bastard to hang. But why would he kill my boy just because I cussed him?"

Then the sheepman began to curse in all earnest. He stood between the graves, one foot propped on the larger mound and the shovel stuck into the smaller to steady himself, and called William Ivey every vile epithet that Youngblood had ever heard. The sheepman never used the name of William Ivey, as if it were made of words unspeakable. To the deputy the cursing was sacriligious, coming from this man standing on the bare graves of his wife and son; but in the earnestness and passion of the curses were something a little akin to tears.

When the man had quieted down, Youngblood said a few words of farewell, which were not answered, and climbed back into the buggy. He guided the mare away from the creek, where the ground was smoother, urged her into a trot, then looked back. The sheepman stood still between the two mounds of red clay on the rise beside the creek, leaning on the long-handled shovel.

He was disturbed but had found further vindication for the course to which he was already committed.

Chapter 8

JUDGE PENDERGRASS finally accepted his brother's repeated invitation, though with misgivings. He had concluded that he and his banker brother could come to no common understanding in the trouble now hovering over Comanche Wells, and he felt that it would be better for their relationship to avoid each other until it was over. Without apologizing or even mentioning his angry behavior during their last interview, Steve had invited the judge several times to come out to his home. Finally, not wishing to appear to hold a grudge, the judge accepted and was picked up at the hotel and carried in style to the Stephen Pendergrass home in a carriage which had been custom built by the Studebaker Wagon Company.

Stephen's home, a half mile west of the main part of town, was a two-storey mansion, painted fresh white, with four large columns at the front. The trees about the house were tall and the lawn was green, a rarity in the dry climate. The banker-rancher and his wife were the only occupants of the house. Their children were gone east. The servants, white and colored, lived in quarters at the rear.

Stephan's wife was a quiet woman, pale as if she had been kept in a closet, with little to say except polite nothings during the elaborate dinner. The judge felt faintly uncomfortable in her presence. He did not trust his brother's hospitality, and yet he felt guilty that he did not. He was relieved that the woman didn't come with them into the library, where Steve had coffee and brandy brought.

"Look at these books, Albert," the big man said. "I don't know why you don't stay here with us when you have a term of court in Comanche Wells. I never have time to read. Most of them haven't been touched in years." He was strolling along by the rows of books with his hands behind his back. The shelves ran around most of three sides of the thirty-foot room, eight feet high. The bindings were rich and elaborate.

The judge swayed along on his crippled leg, studying the titles, thinking about the law library of which he was so fond, amounting to maybe one-tenth as many volumes. "It makes me wish," he said, "I was a banker, instead of a judge."

"A rancher you mean, Albert. That's where the money is if you know what you're doing. There's no money in banking out here. Too many people want to borrow money when they haven't got the guts to make a success. Collateral doesn't mean anything; it's the determination and ability of the man that counts. I made a feller named Long a loan a while back. He used to be sheriff here. He didn't have enough to back up the money, but he's the kind of man that'll make a go of it."

The judge thought of Sheriff Bell's attempt to put Long on as a deputy during the present crisis and of Youngblood's return from the Long ranch with a bruised cheek and black eye, but he said nothing about it. "You have a beautiful library, Steve," he said.

69

"You're welcome to borrow any book you want to any time," the big man said. "You know that. Albert, I'm glad we're here in the library, because I've got something to say to you, and this is a good place to start. You're a man of books. But I think a man of books makes a big mistake sometimes."

"How's that?"

"He's apt to believe he's the only man that does any thinking. Don't you look at ranchers sometimes and other men of action and not give them credit for being smart like you are?"

"I don't know, Steve. Maybe I do. I don't think it's a very admirable thing to do, but maybe I do it."

"Well, I want to talk to you on your own terms. About ideas. I don't want to argue but I want to talk to you about this so-called 'trial' we had here, not like you were a judge and me some culprit you were lecturing, but like two thinking men."

The judge shook his head. "I'll discuss it with you, but I may as well tell you now that I don't think any good can come of it. Why can't we just disagree and forget it?"

"Why can't we disagree and discuss it? Are you so much smarter just because you're a judge? Don't you think I could have any ideas worth talking about?"

"I'm sorry. I'm sure you do," the judge said. "What do you have to say about it?"

"Well, start with the jury. Don't you admit that the jury might have been prejudiced?"

The judge sat down in one of the stuffed, leather-covered chairs and mused for a minute. "Every man is prejudiced in one way or another. We took ordinary precautions; for instance, Ivey's lawyer challenged and rejected one prospective juror because he had been a sheepman. The men who finally made up the jury had various backgrounds. Did you know that one of them, a man named Winkler, fought for the Union during the war? They were cattlemen, shopkeepers, farmers. But this is not really the issue, it seems to me; I believe when you bring men into the solemn air of a court and have them understand that justice depends upon their honesty and conscience, that they will rise above petty considerations, for every man needs justice no matter how he

70

makes his living, and every man has in him some natural reverence for justice."

"In other words, you think if you bring a man that's nothing but riff-raff into court, by some magic he'll know the truth."

"No, he may not. And he may not be riff-raff, either. Who's going to say? Do we need another trial to determine who's fit to be a juryman? And who will be the jury of that trial? Some kind of aristocratic council? And where will we get the council? What will we finally appeal to? Force? Force has been the final appeal through thousands of years of human government, but today we are part of a developing system of law resting on a different basis, the idea of equality and the idea that men are able to make just decisions through appeal to their own intelligence and conscience."

"Maybe this development you're talking about is wrong," Stephen said. He was not smiling, and had not smiled since the talk began. "Maybe that's where we're making a mistake, saying that riff-raff is just as good as anybody."

"We hold these truths to be self-evident, that all men are created equal . . ." the judge quoted. "Strangely, Steve, we know that all men are not equal, not even at birth, and yet this faith in the worth of even the sorriest man has a peculiar strength as the basis of law and government. We . . ."

"In other words, we say it even if we know it's not true."

"Well, we make it our public answer to the question of the quality of men, that all men are created equal. I believe that one reason is that by this approach we make it more easily possible for a naturally superior man to fill his proper superior position."

"You say, 'we make it our public answer . . .'"

"Yes."

"But this isn't the public here. In spite of all your fine words, Albert, we both know that some men are just plain riff-raff that have never done themselves or anybody else any good."

The judge smiled and his eyes twinkled. "I'll have to cede you that point. But that doesn't really condemn juries."

"I'll give you a case out of books. What if Columbus had listened to a jury of twelve men to find out whether the world is round or flat? They'd have said it was flat, and he wouldn't have sailed."

"Thats hardly a fair example."

"Why? Because it doesn't jibe with your ideas?"

"No. Because it's quite easy for you to know that the world is round. It's a natural fact, and it's the kind of fact that mankind may take its time in learning. But it's not easy to know the guilt or innocence of a man, and we must find out with relative speed. It's a different . . ."

"I know what you think," the big man said.

"Oh?"

"You think the world being round is a fact, but whether Ivey killed that damned sheepherder kid, that's just opinion."

The judge hesitated. He was inclined to break off the discussion. He was interested in it but had not changed his opinion that no good could come from it. Anyway he couldn't stop here; his brother was indeed a "thinking" man in certain ways. "No, I honestly don't believe that," he said. "I believe society must act upon the fact about the murder, and that our jury system is the best way we have of determining the fact."

"Then you believe it because the jury says it."

"I accept the jury's verdict, yes."

"But, dammit, Albert, you heard the evidence! What do *you* think?"

"Well, I will make it more clear. I *accept* the verdict, and also I personally believe that Ivey murdered the little boy in cold blood."

"Well, at least you've admitted that you're a man and not just some cog in a court system. Would it ever be possible for you to personally believe different from what the jury said?"

"Yes."

"And you would still *accept* the verdict?"

"Yes."

"If you *knew* the verdict was wrong, and the case was important to you, I suppose you'd still accept the verdict?"

The judge studied the proud face of his brother; it was still perfectly serious. The judge chuckled. "You would

72

make a good lawyer, Steve. I don't know about your hypothetical question. I believe that if I knew a verdict was wrong, I would be able to offer convincing evidence to an appeal court."

"In other words you would be bucking a jury verdict?"

"In a legal way. Our system of law is made of more than juries."

"Suppose the whole blooming system is wrong?"

"Well, I don't believe it is. Of course, it's not perfect. And if may be changed. I think you know I helped rewrite the state constitution in '75. I think it's a pretty good piece of work, but it's subject to correction by perfectly legal means."

"Listen, Albert," the big man said. "We're beating around the bush. Let me ask you a question you won't like to answer. If a man knew a verdict was wrong and he couldn't get legal relief, would it ever be right to buck it?"

"I don't mind answering that. 'Ever' is a long time. I can imagine a man's being justified in acting against established authority. That's what George Washington and Thomas Jefferson did."

"I never thought you'd admit it."

"I have no reason not to admit it. But Steve, if you are thinking about joining forces with those who would use violence to get Ivey . . ."

"Listen," the big man interrupted.

"No, you listen to me, and let me tell you something I feel very strongly about, Steve. If you are thinking about helping those who intend to break Ivey out of jail, consider carefully what a man does when he revolts against established authority. He must know the risks and be ready for defeat. He must be cautious of his cohorts, sure of his integrity, sure of the issue he has chosen to stand on. And beyond that, he should be aware of the sweep of history and his place in it."

"Now you're lecturing me. You can't forget you're a judge, can you? Let me say something about your 'sweep of history.' Where was your law when nesters all over the country began eating other men's beef? Stealing one head, ten head, twenty head at a time. I tell you violent methods outside the law have been necessary, and they've been excusable. And they may still be necessary."

73

"No, Steve, violent methods such as Ivey's bush-whacking were never necessary, and they were certainly never excusable. Furthermore such violence always leads to depravity, more and more sordid killing. Civilization cannot be built on such a foundation."

"You're always preaching to me about civilization," the big man said. "Look at this house, this library. Where would your damned courthouse be without my tax money?"

"Justice is established by people, not money. And so is civilization."

"Now, that's a bunch of high sounding words if I ever heard any. Let me tell you something about your idealism, Albert. You warn me about helping Ivey. Let me warn you. Ideas which *cannot* prevail are wrong; I don't care how fancy they sound."

The judge answered calmly, aware that a threat had come into their talk. "But ideas which are otherwise right and *may* prevail are right. Stephen, we've gone far enough with this conversation. It's been interesting, but . . ."

"Listen," the big man said. "I'm going to tell you something that makes all this talk unimportant. I know Ivey is innocent. I'm telling you this as a brother, and I expect you to take my word for it. I know he's innocent."

"How could you know?"

"I know."

"But that doesn't mean anything to me."

"Now you're calling me a liar."

"I'm telling you that I can't act on any such statement. There's no action I could take if I wanted to on such basis."

"You could pull some strings."

"Why should I pull strings? Give me some facts if you've got them. If I act it will be as a judge. Who do you think you are to ask a judge to blindly accept your word, let you be the judge, while he goes about pulling strings?"

"I'm through arguing," Stephen Pendergrass said. "I've got ten-thousand dollars here." He opened a desk drawer, removed a stack of money held together by rubber bands, and pitched it onto the small table beside the judge. "You can use it for expense money. If you need more, you can have more. Lots more. I know Ivey is innocent, and I want that appeal to go through."

The judge was surprised, caught without words for a moment. "You're joking," he finally said, quietly.

"Hell no, I'm not joking."

"So the Association has chosen you to do their bribery."

"The Association has got nothing to do with it, dammit! It's my money, and nobody will know anything about it except you and I."

"What is there about me that makes you think I would take it? You don't think very highly of judges, do you?"

"I think you'll take it because you're not a fool."

"I'm turning it down because I'm not a fool. I've got very little in this world, God knows, except my ideas and my opinion of myself as a judge, and now you ask me to smear all that with crap. You make me sick." The judge was indeed sick, with anger. His hands were trembling, and he felt as if all his blood had gathered in his stomach. "You've had the money there all the time. I've listened to your arguments and respected them, even admired them, and took you at your word that you wanted to talk like brothers trying to get at the heart of our differences, and all the time you had the money there to seduce me with."

The judge picked up the bundle of money and hurled it at his brother, who was standing. The big man did not dodge. The money bundle struck him in the throat, separating and falling around him and in the room behind him.

As the judge swayed his way rapidly toward the door, Stephen said, "Wait, Albert! Don't go out that door! If you go out that door, you needn't come back, because you're no brother of mine." Then seeing that the judge did not stop, he screamed, as he had before, "And don't come crying to me on your knees!"

The judge turned in the door. His voice was quiet in spite of his nervous anger. "I'll be more merciful than that. You may come to me any time you wish. On your knees."

Walking back toward town in the dark, he wished that Steve would relent and send the fancy hack to pick him up, so that he could refuse it. The walking was a comfort to him and he took pride in it. He had forgotten through the years that he looked somewhat ridiculous

75

walking, and only thought of the fact that with his remarkable swaying gait he could go as fast and far as any
man. The walk was more than a comfort to him; it was a
symbol of the progress that a man can make without a
custom-built hack to ride in.

Chapter 9

DEPUTY YOUNGBLOOD thought the drunk smelled more
like rot-gut whisky than any man he had ever smelled.
He reeked with it, seemed to even have it in his hair.
The man's name was Giles and he worked as ramrod on
Underwood's ranch. Andy had brought him in for
breaking a window at McSween's Saloon.

Youngblood noticed a strange look on the man's face
as he shoved him into a cell on the ground floor, on the
other side of the corridor from the sheriff's office.

"I don't want to be in jail by myself," Giles mumbled
thickly. "Ain't you got nobody in jail but me?"

"Lay down and sleep it off," Youngblood told him.

He didn't like the looks of the situation, so he went
around back to the sheriff's quarters and woke up his
superior, who was trying to catch up on sleep he had
lost the last two nights.

"What's the problem?" the sheriff asked. "Let him so-
ber up; then if he won't satisfy McSween on the window,
we'll take him before the J.P."

"I was just wondering if he could have got in jail on
purpose," the deputy said. "I don't know him very well,
but I know Underwood and he's pretty strict. Besides,
you know, it's not payday. What was a foreman doing
in town?"

"Go see what McSween has to say. I'm going to wake
up Slim. It don't sound right to me either."

Youngblood walked down the street toward McSween's
Saloon. The town was pretty calm with no more cattlemen than usual in sight. But if something tricky were
going on, he knew they couldn't expect it to be obvious.

McSween was not excited about the incident. "All I

want," he said, "is another window pane, like I told Andy. I'll put it in myself. I ain't wanting to make no trouble for any cowboy."

"Did you hit him over the head with a bottle of whisky?" Youngblood asked.

"No, I never touched him. I swear to it. Why? Did he say I hit him?"

"No, I just wondered."

"Well, I never touched him. It was Giles and this other cowpoke that done the fighting, or rather scuffling; there wasn't no real fight to it. All I want is another window pane."

"I didn't know there was another man with him," Youngblood said. "Did they come in together?"

"Yeah. They were buddies when they come in. But after Giles threw that glass through the window, his buddy lit a shuck, fast. I ain't making no complaint, Youngblood. If he'll get me another window pane, I'll be happy."

"Did Giles get some whisky spilled on him, in his hair or some place?"

"No. And I didn't hit him, Youngblood. I didn't touch him."

"How much did they drink?"

"Why, they were drunk when they come in here. You know, yelling and talking loud. I never served them but one drink. Then this other cowpoke stepped on Giles foot, and they got to shoving and swinging at each other, too drunk to do much damage. When Giles throwed the glass, he missed him a half a mile. How come all the questions, Youngblood? I ain't trying to make no trouble, except to get me a window pane, and I got a witness on that. Annie Lee was in here and she seen it."

"You'll get your window pane," Youngblood told him. He thought of asking the bartender whether the fight might have been put-on, but decided he had all the evidence he needed, and there was no use in betraying his suspicions to the talkative McSween.

He was heading back toward the courthouse when he noticed a familiar skinny, white-haired figure in the lobby of the Robert Lee Hotel. The man had gone upstairs by the time Youngblood got inside, but he was sure the man was Underwood. The clerk affirmed that Mr. Underwood had registered that morning.

No horses with the Underwood brand were tied on main street. Youngblood decided to do a little more investigating before reporting back to the sheriff. He walked down to the stagecoach barns, where most of the town's livery stable business was done, and asked a few questions. An Underwood hand had brought in five saddle horses that morning and had asked that they not be turned loose in the livery stable's ten-acre pasture to graze, but be fed oats and kept up ready. "And a mule too, Mr. Youngblood," the stable boy said. "All done up with a pack, with grub and everything like somebody was going prospecting. The pack is over yonder in the harness shed with the saddles."

He headed back toward the courthouse, walking fast. When he came back onto main street, the smell of smoke like cloth burning struck his nostrils, and he saw it streaming out the door of the sheriff's office and one upstairs window. He started running.

Andy and Slim were running from the well in the back with two sloshing buckets apiece. Inside, the sheriff and the judge were dragging a choking, gasping prisoner, Giles, into the front office.

"You damn fool!" the sheriff said. "I hope you got plum full of smoke!"

Andy and Slim went into the cell on the ground floor where Giles had been kept. Youngblood ran straight up the stairs to check on Ivey.

"Let me out of this damn stinking rat hole!" Ivey said. "You aim to let me burn to death?"

"It's just a little smoke," the deputy told him. Ivey kept yelling as the deputy looked around to make sure that everything was all right.

Downstairs he found that Andy and Slim had finished stomping out the burning mattress, which had been the source of all the smoke. Giles was still coughing and his eyes were red.

"You set that mattress afire on purpose," the sheriff charged. "Now you got to pay the county for a mattress besides paying McSween for a window."

"You searched this man, didn't you, Sheriff?" the judge asked.

"Yes, and I'm going to search him again. He ain't going to keep any matches on him, that's for sure. Andy, go over him again. Take his boots off."

Giles was sullen. He didn't seem as drunk as he had seemed before. "How am I going to light a smoke?" he asked.

"You ain't going to do no smoking, mister," the sheriff said as he shoved him into the cell beside the one he had been in before.

Youngblood went over with the sheriff and judge the information he had gathered at McSween's and the livery stable. It didn't add up to much that was definite.

"Sounds to me like they might be figuring on sending Ivey toward Mexico. A mule and a pack of grub would come in handy," the sheriff said.

"And Giles is suppose to help in the break some way," the judge put in. "But how?"

"Maybe he is just finding out the lay of the land—where Ivey is kept."

"Maybe," the judge admitted. "Of course, they could have found that out from that dude lawyer; he was in yesterday. Or maybe he wouldn't take part in any such scheme. I don't know."

"Judge, I been thinking something over several days," the sheriff said. "I haven't made up my mind about it, but what do you think? Reckon we ought to take Ivey out of here? Move him to another jail?"

"I've been expecting you to bring that up."

"Why?"

"Well," the judge laughed, "because you're a practical man. I've been thinking about it too. It's a hard question. It sort of comes down to the question of whether we are able to carry out the law here in Carroll County, or whether we have to admit that we cannot, and have to sneak our prisoner out at night and take him somewhere else. Frankly, I wouldn't be happy taking him to another jail unless we brought him back here to execute the sentence. I think he ought to hang right out there in the open place beside the jail in broad daylight."

"I was afraid you'd say that," the sheriff said.

"Why?"

It was the sheriff's turn to laugh. "I mean I figured you'd say it. You knew I'd bring it up because I'm a practical man. I don't know what kind of a man to call you, Judge, but I figured you'd want to hang him here."

"Well, what do you personally think?"

"Danged if I don't agree with you," the sheriff said. "I'd much rather hang him here, if we can *do* it."

"Well, we take a risk if we move him, too. Where would be the best place to take him if we were going to do it? Briggsburg?"

"I think so," the sheriff said.

"Well, you have no stage line, unless you go clear around by Colorado City. Suppose you send two deputies cross-country with him. It's over a hundred miles."

Youngblood interrupted. "I believe I could take him by myself if you all decide to send him. With a pair of handcuffs I could handle him."

"Unless about six men jumped you," the sheriff said.

"And Ivey would be missed. If nobody saw you leave, at least his lawyer would find out about it," the judge said. "You'd have the trip there, and then if you brought him back at the end of the month, you'd have the trip back, right through all those ranches. Then you'd have a problem in Briggsburg. There's nothing to keep a bunch of cattlemen from going up there after him."

"I'll go along with you, Judge," the sheriff said. "I just thought I'd bring it up."

"Then let's keep him here. I tell you what I'll do, though. Have you had any luck yet rounding up any more deputies?"

"Not a danged bit."

"Well, I'm going to telegraph Ranger headquarters, and the Governor, too, and see if we can get a little help out here. You might pick out a stand-by posse of townspeople; they could be a big help if you select men who will follow instructions." The judge seemed to have his mind on something else. He pinched his jaws together with one hand and seemed to be staring at something a mile away through his brass-rimmed spectacles. "How in the hell could Giles help a jail break by getting in jail? Could he have a hacksaw blade, maybe in his belt or in a boot top?"

"Go over him again," the sheriff said to this three deputies.

The judge had guessed right. When they took the boots

off Giles, who had become belligerent by this time, Youngblood saw at once that the stitching had been cut at the top of one boot. He brought it into the sheriff's office and pulled three hacksaw blades from between the lining and the outer leather.

"That dirty skunk," the sheriff said. "I ought to make him eat those things."

"I believe I'd bring Underwood in here and let him face up to this," the judge said. "He pretends to be a responsible citizen. I'd like to see what he's got to say."

"Get him," the sheriff said to Youngblood.

The deputy headed back for the Robert Lee Hotel. He thought about how many men had come to town with Underwood; there were five saddled horses, one of which had been for Ivey and one for Giles. That left one for Underwood, one for the other cowpoke who had been in the put-up fight at McSween's, and one for still another man. The hotel clerk answered his question by pointing into the dining room. Youngblood felt relieved at finding the rancher eating supper with two cowpokes; he felt sure that he was facing all that there was to face right now in the situation.

"Mr. Underwood, the sheriff wants to see you," he said.

The white-haired man looked up, surprised and immediately angry. He had a lined face and sunken mouth that puckered like that of an old woman, but his eyes were hard and unblinking. "What for?" he asked.

"For investigation."

"That don't mean nothing to me."

"Maybe not," Youngblood said. "But you'll have to come with me."

"I will not. Seems to me like the law is getting mighty high-handed around here lately."

"I don't want to pull a gun on you, Mr. Underwood, but you're going with me down to see the sheriff." He kept his eyes on the old man and still remained aware of every movement of the two cowpokes. They seemed to be unarmed.

"Am I under arrest?"

"Yes sir. I can't speak for the sheriff, but I think he just wants to talk to you, him and the judge."

"All right, I'll be down there after while."

"No sir, you'll have to come with me now, Mr. Un-

81

derwood." His right hand hung limp beside the wooden handle of his .44.

The old man stared at him for a moment, rose slowly, and said to the other two, "Wait here. I'll be back." It was as if he were saying, Don't do anything.

Back at the courthouse, the sheriff let the judge do the talking. The judge fixed the old man with a gaze and a manner like that of a teacher scolding a schoolboy. "George Underwood, I'd like to know what you have to say for yourself in regard to this little plan you're engaged in, You claim to be a sincere member of the Baptist Church; you have strict rules of decorum for your employees; and now you take part in a totally irresponsible and sneaking scheme like this."

The white-headed man was taken aback, but met the judge's gaze squarely. "I don't know what you're talking about," he said.

"And now you stand there before God and everybody and lie about it," the judge went on. He shook his forefinger at him. "George Underwood, you ought to be ashamed of yourself."

"What are you talking about?"

"You know very well what I'm talking about. We know all about the put-up fight, and your horses and pack mule ready to go, and the hacksaw blades." He picked up the metal strips from the sheriff's desk and slapped them down again. "What we don't understand is how a man like you would be a part of such a thing."

"You don't have no evidence on me, or Giles neither."

"We have plenty of circumstantial evidence to know what you were planning to do. You expected to send Ivey to Mexico. What I can't understand is how such a respectable man as you could stoop so low."

Underwood seemed to need to explain himself, but no weakness showed in his voice. "Before the first of August, you'll wish Ivey was got out of here some sneaky way. They don't agree, the cattlemen; they can't get together. But they agree on one thing: Ivey's going to be took out of here, and no mistake. If he ain't got out some easy way, they's some that means to tear this building down rock by rock and kill every highhanded lawman in Carroll County. And they can do it; mark my word."

82

"And so," the judge said, "because someone else means to do something wrong, that excuses any irresponsible, lowdown action of yours or any lies you want to tell."

Underwood would say no more. The sheriff released Giles on the promise that the mattress would be paid for and McSween would be satisfied. As the white-haired man went out the door with his ramrod, the judge said, winking at Youngblood, "George Underwood, I hope your conscience bothers you about this. And if you'll think about it, you'll be ashamed of yourself."

The stern lines of Underwood's face never broke.

Chapter 10

YOUNGBLOOD had sat there in the sheriff's office and listened to the pounding outside for half an hour. His consciousness was tuned to sounds inside the building, especially up toward Ivey's cell, and sounds from the street. He had been halfway dreaming about Lila, wondering how she passed the days. Finally he asked himself, Who could be hammering out there? and went out to see. In the clear area at the end of the courthouse facing away from town, he saw Elmer Cobb, the little husband of Maggie Cobb, the cook. The man was working around the wagonload of new timber the sheriff had bought; already he had spiked together four pieces for the beginning of a square platform.

The deputy walked out to where the little man was working. "What are you doing, Mr. Cobb? Did the sheriff say to start on this?"

"Well, he hired me. He hired me to do it."

"I know he hired you, but he doesn't want it done till he gives you the word. Didn't he tell you that?"

"Yes, he told me that. He did. But I don't have any other work to do, so I thought I'd get started, you might say."

"Well, he doesn't want it done now, and he has a reason for waiting. You'll have to stop and tear these timbers apart."

Cobb was an innocent looking man with a prominent Adam's apple and the gift of appearing surprised at even the plainest event. A ne'er-do-well, he was thoroughly dominated by his sloppy wife Maggie. At intervals he "went on the wagon" for a few days, the number depending on how long it took him to earn a few dollars at odd jobs as a carpenter. "Well, I don't know," he said. "I needed something to do, and I just didn't think maybe the sheriff would mind."

Maggie came from the rear of the building and entered the conversation. "Mr. Cobb has gone on the wagon," she announced. "He's got to have something to do to take his mind off of bad things, so we thought . . ."

"Maggie," Youngblood said, "you know how strict the sheriff is about people following orders. Now, he doesn't want this thing built yet." He turned to the little carpenter. "Knock those timbers apart and get them back on that stack. And I hope you get it done before the sheriff wakes up."

"Mr. Cobb has gone on the wagon for good this time," Maggie whined. "And he needs something to do, and we didn't think it would hurt . . ."

"Yes, I have," Cobb said. "Sure enough. I'm on it for good now."

"Didn't the sheriff tell you to build a pine box too?" Youngblood asked

"Yes, he did. Yes."

"Have you got the lumber?"

"Yes, it's out in the shed."

"Did the sheriff tell you exactly what he wants?"

"Uh . . . Two by two by seven feet. And a lid."

"All right. Soon as you put these timbers back on the pile where you got them, you can build the box. But build it in the shed, and leave it in the shed."

As he turned to go, Maggie spoke up again. "Mr. Youngblood, I've about got Mr. Ivey's dinner ready, and I wonder if you'd mind if I took it to him. I'm sure the sheriff wouldn't mind."

"No, Maggie, we settled that for good. The sheriff *would* mind and *does* mind. You're not to go upstairs."

"Well, I don't think the sheriff would mind just once. I haven't even seen Mr. Ivey in two weeks, and I want

84

to ask him how he likes his dinner cooked. The poor man."

"No deal, Maggie," he said and turned his back to avoid further argument. He was half amused and half disgusted. It was a good thing he had come out to look and had stopped Cobb before he went any further. The sheriff had thought about building the scaffold inside the courthouse, even though it would have meant tearing out some ceiling and a partition. The judge had felt it would be better to build it out in the open, and his idea had prevailed. But both of them had agreed that it should not be started before the appeal was heard from; there was no point in betraying their certainty that the appeal would be denied.

Back in the sheriff's office, Youngblood heard pounding and muffled shouts from upstairs. He went up to Ivey's cell. The prisoner was standing up gripping the bars. "What's all that hammering out there, Youngblood?"

"That's just Elmer Cobb," the deputy told him.

"What's he building?"

"He's working on the corral fence. Why?"

"It don't sound to me like in the direction of the corral fence."

"Well, if you're not going to take my word, why do you ask me?"

"I don't know, Youngblood. I've done lost all my sense of direction penned up here in this damned rat hole. I don't even know which way town is from here. If I just had me a window so's I could look out." The prisoner pulled backward and forward, testing his muscles against the bars. He was so pale that the scar on his forehead, which ran down through one eyebrow, was barely visible in the dim light.

"Youngblood, you ain't like the sheriff," he went on. "You wouldn't pen a man up like a dog this way just to spite him. Let me come out there in the hall and walk up and down and the sheriff won't never know. Just let me get some exercise and look out the window once."

The deputy said, "Look, Ivey, you know I can't do that. And if you don't stop calling me up here without any reason, I'm going to stop coming at all. You're going to mess yourself up with me, good."

"You could treat me decent if you wanted to. Damn

85

you! You're worse than the sheriff. Wait, Youngblood! Don't go off. Wait!"

"I'll bring your dinner up pretty soon if you'll quiet down," the deputy told him, heading back downstairs.

For the past few days Youngblood had been taking turns with the sheriff at sleeping. The deputy would spend up to eight hours each day sleeping, eight hours on duty with the sheriff, and eight hours handling the sheriff's duties. He had found that the sheriff would back him up in any decision he made. Andy and Slim were taking care of the patrols in town and any errands outside town. Youngblood was glad that the sheriff was in the office with him when they had the visitor, Mr. Stephen Pendergrass, that afternoon.

The banker came in with more of a scowl than usual on his dignified face. "Sheriff," he announced, "there's a damn greaser down town I think you better pick up and put in jail."

"Oh?" the sheriff said. "What's he doing?"

"I don't know, but he's up to no good. He's been watching me and watching the bank."

"What's his name?"

"Someone said his name's Torres. I don't know. You're the one that's supposed to do the investigating around here. Not me."

"Well, I don't know, Mr. Pendergrass," the sheriff said. "If he hasn't done anything, I can't hardly throw him in jail. It's not against the law just to hang around town. Isn't he a friend of yours?"

"What do you mean 'a friend of mine'?" The banker seemed honestly surprised. "Of course he's not. I don't know what you mean. And I don't know what we pay all these taxes for to support the sheriff's department, if we can't get a little protection. If you can't put him in jail without a charge, you can at least run him out of town. You've got the authority to do that, haven't you?"

Youngblood knew what was running through the sheriff's mind. The suggestion that the Mexican be put in jail seemed to indicate another plot such as the one executed by Underwood, where Giles got himself in jail on purpose. But the suggestion that the Mexican be run out of town was something else again. They knew Torres was Ivey's friend, and that Pendergrass was on Ivey's

86

side; yet the banker seemed honestly anxious to be rid of the Mexican, as if he didn't know the Mexican was Ivey's friend.

"We'll keep an eye on the man, Mr. Pendergrass," the sheriff said.

"Young man," the banker said to Youngblood, "if you'll step outside, I'd like to have a short word with you."

Out in the street, the big man's face seemed to soften slightly; he almost seemed to wish to be agreeable. "You were going to think over my offer of a job. What did you decide?"

"Well, I don't know Mr. Pendergrass. It sure is a hard decision. I just can't seem to make up my mind."

"I don't see why not, young man. What's the hold-up? You'll never get very far in this world if you can't make up your mind."

"Well, you see, I would be better off in wages if I worked for you, Mr. Pendergrass, but I just hate to quit the sheriff when he has problems and he would be short handed."

"Your duty is to yourself. The sheriff's problems are his own. Like I told you before, if you're really a cattle-man at heart, you'll want to make sure you're on the right side, and you haven't got forever to make up your mind. You've got to decide, or you may find the offer is closed. I'll pay you fifty-five a month, and that's as high as I'll go."

"Well, I'll be thinking about it, Mr. Pendergrass."

The banker snorted as he turned and headed up the street.

Youngblood went in and reported the second bribe offer to his superior. Slim had come into the office; he commented, "Youngblood, next time that banker brings that up, you see if you can't get me in on some of that gravy. Tell him I ain't near as hard to deal with as you are."

The judge was surprised to see his brother coming down the courthouse corridor toward his office. He smiled dryly and asked, "Are you lost?"

Stephen responded with a question. "What's that supposed to mean?"

"Well, from your remarks when I left your house last

87

week, I gathered that you would not seek my company again." He held the door open for his brother, without any verbal invitation, and closed it behind him.

"I come out of pity, Albert," the big man said. "I come out of pity. And this will be the last time."

"I'm afraid your pity will be wasted. In fact I'm quite sure you are wasting your time and my time. Stephen, why do you press this matter? Why won't you let it drop? We have already gone too far, you and I, and it will be a miracle if we ever feel like brothers again."

"This is the last time," the big man repeated. "I just want to make sure that you see yourself for what you are. You preached to me about my 'cohorts' and the issues I 'stand on.' I just want to make sure you see yourself as I see you."

They stood ten feet apart in the office. Neither had any inclination to sit. There was no friendliness in their words. The judge stood waiting. "Well?" he asked.

"The political power of this state is changing. You understand that all too well; you're a politician, Albert; I don't care how many fancy, high-minded ideas you may have about yourself, you're a politician and nothing more. The rabble are trying to take over this state, the Grangers; they almost have the legislature already. These are the people you are siding with."

The judge was smiling faintly.

"They remind me of a bunch of saddle tramps riding the grub line," his brother went on. "After we've conquered the land and made it safe for them, they sneak into the cattle country and squat; they can't make a living farming so they steal beef to eat. Or they set up in town to cheat cowboys out of their wages. They expect to take power, not because by-God they deserve it in any way, but because of their numbers. They're like flies pestering a steer. And you take sides with them."

The judge kept his little smile. "You may as well know that I don't take your arguments very seriously, Steve. I found out the other night that ideas or ideals don't mean much to you; you want your way, that's all. Like a child, you want your way. But I will say this: if wanting to bring this murderer to justice puts me on some 'side' in your books, well, that's that."

"I think you're a coward," the big man said. "This

88

isn't the first time I've seen you take the cowardly side. You're a traitor to the ranchers today, and you were a traitor to your state and the South during the war."

"Yes, I was a traitor and Sam Houston was a traitor. Lee was almost a traitor; he fought a hard battle with himself before he quit the Union and went back to Virginia. But you know my failing, Steve? I wasn't enough of a traitor. I was too much content to keep my mouth shut and let my people follow a path I knew to be wrong. If this state had held six men like Houston in those days, we would never have left the Union, and if this country had held enough men with his vision and strength, we would have avoided a great deal of sorrow; we would have skipped the blackest page in American history. I learned a hard lesson from the war, Steve: if a man believes something is right and he believes it is a critical issue, let him stand up and fight for it; merely to be right is not enough."

The judge's faint smile turned into a grin. "But I am letting you drag me into an argument again. And your arguments are as unfounded as ever, Steve. One moment you accuse me of being a political hypocrite who follows the trend for his own advantage; the next moment you remind me of my position on secession. You know as well as I do that my position in those days amounted to political suicide. I have seen my old colleagues in the Attorney General's chair, yes, even in the Governor's mansion; one of my junior law partner's sits on the Court of Criminal Appeals. And here I am, a judge in a frontier district, with little hope of going further. Well, that's all right; at least they are going to say that you can get justice in Pendergrass' district."

"Pendergrass' district!" the big man scoffed. "You and your two-bit job as a judge! You sure are a fool, Albert. How in the Sam Hill do you think you can hold Ivey?"

"I'm not a big enough fool to tell you how. But we can do it."

"You haven't got a chance," the big man said. "Listen, Albert, I know who's the power behind this plot to get Ivey. It's you. Nobody but you. Without you, Sheriff Bell would knuckle under. And what chance have you got. You're a God damned weakling and a cripple. I could knock you through that wall with one hand."

The judge was still smiling. He had noticed often through the years that people avoided mentioning his game leg, even went out of their way to keep from helping him. He had wondered at other people's sensitivity about it; they seemed to think that if attention were called to it, he would burst out crying. And at times he had thought, damn such an attitude. Now, to his brother, he jibed, "See me running! Watch me trying to get under my desk so you won't hurt me! Yes, I'm a cripple. You hated to admit when we were young that I was as good a man as you were in the childish things we did; and you hate to admit it now, but we have put away childish things, and I am still as good a man as you are. I had the privilege of talking to your friend, Mr. Underwood, the other day, and I told him he ought to be ashamed of himself. I say the same thing to you: God knows you ought to be ashamed of yourself. You have fallen so low as to threaten to knock a man down because you think he is a cripple. But that's not the only way you have fallen, Steve.

"I didn't mean to talk to you seriously at all today," the judge went on, "but let me beg you: look at yourself. You are soiling your hands. You are stooping to something beneath you. Give up this sordid fight and let those who are really guilty take their medicine. You are above it; the other ranchers are above it. Let Ivey and the man who paid him to kill reap what they have sown. For God's sake wash your hands of it; it's unworthy of you."

Something in the words of the judge had struck deeply into Stephen Pendergrass and he responded with his characteristic quick anger. He towered over the judge, spluttering, almost incoherently. "You're a fool!"

The judge was not coerced. "I know one thing, Steve. Our talks about this matter have not been pleasant, and this one has revealed nothing new. If you approach me again in this mood, you may find, not a brother, but a judge. I'm growing tired of your vulgarity and your bribes and your threats."

"You damn fool!" the big man said at the office door. "What could you do? It would be your word against mine."

"I might convict you by trickery. I might hide a wit-

90

ness in the closet. I am sure enough tired of your attitude, Steve."

The big man slammed the door as he had done once before, and the ceilings and partitions of the entire courthouse reverberated.

The judge smiled faintly at the petty characteristic display of anger; the smile faded. He felt a little anger himself, but the dominant note of his feeling about the break between them was sadness. Steve was his closest, almost his only, living relative. He had never been jealous of the big man's success, but proud, knowing what it had taken in ability and hard work. The tie between them in recent years had been tentative, based on the past and perhaps on some possible potential need for brotherhood. The judge had never felt dependency on him, rather had felt some less alone in the world through having a worthy brother.

But that which Steve offended in the judge was not tentative nor potential. The law to the judge was mistress and living wife and children and home and even God. He never told anyone what the law meant to him. Out of the barrenness of his life he seized upon it and made it everything. His feeling was not a thing coupled with great ambition but was rather a fierce desire to make actual the abstract and ideal. He had come nearest to expressing it in the words: "they are going to say that you can get justice in Pendergrass' district," but this did not hint at what he meant by "justice." He meant more than a man's getting his deserts, good or bad. For him justice was quite akin to truth. Every simple court case settled properly was a vindication and a justification of the tradition of developing law which he served as a disciple and an apostle. And the simplest case, too, dealing with actual people in their weaknesses, might be a symbol of the way in which all things, each in its proper place, may exist in harmony.

He was uncertain and humble before his great mistress, but little likely to be cowed by wealth or position or any other of the myriad lesser forces in the world.

Youngblood could see that the rider was his uncle so he stood waiting in the street until the rider drew up and dismounted.

"You're not a very hard man to find," Charlie Moss said, laughing.

"How's Lila?"

"She's all right. I had to make a solemn promise I would look you up the first thing when I got to town. Man, am I hot and thirsty! Come in and have a drink."

They were in front of the hotel. Charlie Moss tied his horse to the rail. Youngblood said, "I'll go in with you if you'll sit at a table, and talk to you while you have a drink. No I'll do better than that; I'll buy us some supper. That jail food is getting old."

His uncle pulled an envelope from his shirt pocket. "Here's something you might want." The envelope was sealed and said on the front: Deputy Bart Youngblood. It was the fine handwriting of his wife. From it came the elusive hint of perfume.

"You really think she's all right, Uncle Charlie? I mean, you think she's happy out there and not worried too much?"

His uncle laughed as they went into the hotel. "I think if you'll read that letter you'll know more about it than I could tell you. But I got a kind of a hunch what it says."

When Youngblood had slit the envelope and removed the folded paper, his uncle said suddenly, "Let me see that." He held the envelope to his nose. "Well, I'll be darned! If that isn't just like a woman. I smelled that thing all the way to town and kept looking around for flowers." He handed it back.

The letter read:

> My Dearest Bart,
>
> Your uncle and aunt are as good to me as anyone could be. They try to amuse me and keep me from being lonely, but in spite of everything this is the saddest time of my life.
>
> I keep thinking that it is a hard time for both of us and that we make it harder by being apart. In the day I tell myself you will come through safely, but at night I see you dying in the dusty street in Comanche Wells, and I am not there.
>
> If I could come back to town I would go

to bed at eight o'clock and do everything as you think I should. I know you cannot keep regular hours, but I had rather be near you even if I don't see you often.

I think my time is almost here. Please let me come back home.

Lila

Youngblood folded the letter slowly, replaced it in the envelope, and put it in his shirt pocket. He asked his uncle, "You say you've got a hunch what it says?"

"Yeah, I think I have."

"Does she cry?"

"Well, uh . . ." Charlie Moss laughed a little, "I wasn't going to say anything about it, but, yes, she does. But you know how a pregnant woman is, sort of silly, you know."

"No, I don't guess I do know, Uncle Charlie. Did Aunt Annie . . . I mean . . . Well, did Aunt Annie ever cry that way?"

"No," the older man admitted. "But she ate pickles. She ate peach pickles and beet pickles and cucumber pickles and everything she could get that tasted like pickles. Couldn't get enough of them."

They were halfway through supper before Youngblood asked, "What do you think I ought to do? You think she is just being silly?"

His uncle chewed thoughtfully. "I can't tell you what to do. Nobody knows that but you. She's not just being silly; or maybe she is, but not the way you mean; the fact is, that little girl thinks the sun rises and sets in you. Boy, if you was half the man she thinks you are, you would be something." After a moment's further thought, he said, "I'll tell you what; if you want to bring her back to town, I believe Annie will come with her. That might help."

"That would really help, but, you know, I don't know when I can go get her. I'm on duty twenty-four hours a day now. The sheriff can't hire any more hands, and I hate to ask him for a half a day off."

"You give the word, boy, and I'll bring her."

"I don't know what I'd do without you, Uncle Charlie."

"Don't you worry about that, boy," the older man said.

93

"Listen, just don't let any of these big-shot ranchers like Underwood, or Bledsoe, or Steve Pendergrass—these fellers that think they own the country—just don't let them hornswoggle you. You stand up to them, and if I can do any little thing for you, let me know."

Before Youngblood headed back to his duties, he and his uncle agreed that Lila would be brought back to Comanche Wells as soon as it was convenient for the rancher to bring her. The deputy felt happier about it than he had in weeks.

Chapter 11

THE SECURITY ARRANGEMENTS set up by the sheriff for the purpose of holding Ivey were definite by now. It was felt that the most important thing, at least until the appeal was heard from, was to keep tabs on who was in town. To this end, either Andy or Slim checked the Robert Lee Hotel register and the livery stable at least once a day; the stage was met as it came in on Mondays and Thursdays; saddle horses and buckboards or other vehicles tied on the streets were checked and indentified as to owner.

Another thing held to be important was that each of the four lawmen know the whereabouts of each of the others at all times. All of them now slept around in the rear of the courthouse building in the sheriff's living quarters. It was also necessary that each of them knew exactly what he was responsible for. Youngblood's most important responsibility was to be in the Sheriff's Office during the eight hours the sheriff allotted for himself to sleep; the deputy was to be in the office, or at least in command of the entrance there. The jail portion of the upstairs had been securely boarded off from other portions of the upper storey of the building. Only one flight of stairs went up to the cell block where Ivey was kept and this flight began in the corridor beside the sheriff's office. Since the door between the office and the corridor had been removed, the stairs were always in view.

The evening when Youngblood ate supper at the hotel with Charlie Moss, Slim was asleep back in the quarters; Andy had been sent out to the *cantina* to see if Torres were still in town; Youngblood had walked uptown during the time assigned him for sleeping, and he expected to do one more small duty at the jail before turning in. The sheriff himself was supposed to be in command of that all-important entrance, the stairs toward Ivey. He admitted this later, with wry remorse, and said he was glad that it was he who had been careless instead of one of his deputies. He had walked along the long corridor, up the stairs, and down the short corridor to the judge's office "for a minute" which had lengthened into several minutes; it was that "one little careless act" they had been guarding against.

The sheriff had changed his rule about carrying a gun upstairs near Ivey. It was a chance they had to take. Their sideguns were too precious to remove; if a lawman could not prevent a prisoner in a cell from taking a gun away from him, then they had no chance to hold Ivey anyway. Besides having them for other uses, each of them needed a gun to summon the one or two other lawmen who would always be on the premises.

Youngblood returned to the courthouse, expecting to be in the office when Ivey was fed. They hadn't been strict about it, but it was a good idea to have two men there at that time. Either he or the sheriff would take up the tray, and the other would wait below.

When he opened the door, he saw that the office was empty. Some sound came from upstairs, but it was nothing to warn him. He went from habit toward the stairs, to check. When he was halfway across the office, the pounding of heavy boots came on the stairs, and he saw them. Because they were all he could see, his attention was focused on them, but in the same second he was realizing to whom they belonged, the man came hurtling down on him. The boots belonged to William Ivey.

Later he wondered why he hadn't grabbed for his gun. If he had only been alert, surely he could have triggered off one shot, if not at Ivey, at least into the floor.

The prisoner hit him like a charging bull, with the speed he had gained in the half-run, half-dive down the stairs. The wind went out of the deputy in the collision, and they rolled together across the pine floor. Ivey was

95

shaken, too, but recovered to rise toward the gun rack. On it were six rifles, loaded.

Youngblood swung his leg blindly, and Ivey was upset again. One rifle fell, butt against the floor, out of the prisoner's reach.

Then began a test of strength as the deputy flung his arms around his opponent and yelled at the top of his voice, "Sheriff! Sheriff! Help, Slim!" He was getting his wind back and recovering from his surprise. He knew that his yells were not as loud as they should be to carry, but it was taking everything he had to hang onto the bucking Ivey. The prisoner had amazing strength to have been in jail these long weeks.

He knew he had to hang on, work Ivey away from the fallen rifle, then roll away and make a grab for his own gun. He had to get off a shot; Ivey might have some help coming down the stairs right now. Then the deputy ran into more problems: the prisoner's swinging elbow hit him in the cheek. He lurched closer against him and pinned the man's arms. Ivey twisted and rolled; Youngblood followed relentlessly and pinned him solidly, beside the fallen rifle.

The deputy worked his right hand, pulling hard against their combined weight, around toward the .44 on his hip. Ivey felt the release of the right arm and he thrust himself aside like a spring uncoiling. His movement knocked the rifle completely to the floor. The shifting of Ivey's weight allowed Youngblood to cup his hand around the handle of his pistol and draw it two inches out of its holster; he was still laying halfway on the gun, but he shrank away from it as well as he could and pulled the trigger. The explosion seemed to lift him off of the floor; he thought for a moment he had blown his own leg off.

At the same time, Ivey in his thrashing had brought his hand down directly on the barrel of the rifle. He swung it in a savage arc level with the floor toward the stubborn deputy's head.

Youngblood got one hand up to help break the blow. Even so the stock splintered against his forehead. He was halfway stunned. Ivey scrambled up and broke for the door.

The deputy's hand streaked automatically for his hip and came up empty. His .44 had slid out of its holster. He staggered up and lurched toward the prisoner. The door had been almost closed; the split second it took Ivey to jerk it open and go out was enough to allow Youngblood to get to the door. They tugged momentarily at the door, Ivey outside, the deputy inside. When Ivey released it, Youngblood fell backward.

Now his eyes swept the room for his gun. He was afraid, dizzy as he was, that he couldn't catch Ivey on foot. He scooped it up and ran out the door. The prisoner was not in sight.

The corner of the building was some thirty feet away. He sprinted toward it and saw Ivey disappearing around the rear corner. Youngblood's head was clearing. As he came around the rear corner, he saw that his quarry was no more than fifty feet ahead of him, pounding toward the corral. "Halt you son-of-a-bitch!" he yelled, almost hoping the man would not. He triggered off a shot at the top plank of the corral, and his slug left a white blaze in the wood in front of Ivey's eyes. The deputy was thinking, "If he climbs that fence, I'm going to let him have it," but Ivey did not. He stopped with his hands against the fence, then turned slowly.

They faced each other, panting. Ivey finally said, "Looks like you got me."

"Looks that way, doesn't it."

"I figure our little fight was even," the prisoner said. "You got the advantage now, but you had that gun to start with. Anyway, I'll say you're tougher than I had you figured."

"Let's go," the deputy said.

"Hell no! let's wait a minute. It sure feels good to be outside again."

"Ivey, you give me just one little bit of trouble, and I'm going to put a slug through your shoulder."

"What's that pile of timbers for, Youngblood?"

"None of your damned business. Get going."

The sheriff came running from toward the front of the building and Slim from the quarters in the rear at the same time. The sheriff was bug-eyed when he saw Ivey. "What in the hell, Youngblood?" he yelled. "What in God's name?"

"That's what I'd like to know," the deputy said. "I came back from eating supper at the hotel and when I came into the office he jumped me. He came real close to getting away, too. He might have made it if there had

97

been a horse tied in front of the jail or even across the street."

The sheriff demanded of the prisoner, "How'd you get out?"

Ivey grinned.

"You get smart and I'm going to split your skull with gun barrel," the sheriff said. "Get going. We'll find out."

The sheriff and Slim preceeded the prisoner and Youngblood up the stairs to the cell, where they found Maggie Cobb, half-terrified, the big ring of keys in her hand. "He said he only wanted to get some exercise," she stuttered. "I didn't think it would hurt anything. I didn't know they would be any shooting."

The sheriff snatched the keys and asked, "Can anybody explain to me how any living human can be so God-damned stupid?"

"He only wanted to get some exercise and look out the window. That's what he said. I didn't think it would hurt."

"So you came upstairs against my strict orders, and like that wasn't enough, you went down and stole the keys out of my desk and threw open the cell and turned him out, and you didn't think it would hurt." The sheriff threw wide his arms with the words "turned him out" and glared at her.

The sloppy old woman was sniffling. "He wanted out so bad. The poor man."

"Maggie, hasn't it ever got through to you that this man is sentenced to hang? Get out of here! I don't want to talk to you now. It's against the law to stomp a woman with cowboy boots on." He slammed the door on Ivey and said, "Boy, you've fouled your nest now. You thought you had it rough in that little cell; now I've got to make it even rougher. You'll be sorry for this day."

"Don't call me 'boy,' you chicken bastard," Ivey said. "I've known all along you wanted to make it as rough on me as you could."

"Think what you please, boy, but I'm putting irons on you tomorrow. This ain't going to happen again."

Downstairs, Andy had come in, and the sheriff talked to his three deputies. "It was my fault. I wasn't where I belonged. I'm glad it wasn't one of you fellers. I don't know what to do with that woman. What can you do with a woman like that?" The three deputies were grinning, and the sheriff grinned too. "At least we can try to make sure it don't happen again. I've got two keys to the cells upstairs. Here's one of them Youngblood. Keep it on you. If anybody gets this one off of me, I'm going to be dead first. And we'll take Ivey down to the blacksmith shop tomorrow and get some leg irons on him. Fact is, I'm glad we've got an excuse to do it; it won't be near so easy for anybody to get him away from here. One more thing, Youngblood mentioned what if there had been a horse tied out in front. I'm making a rule; no horses tied in front of this jail; they'll have to be left down the street or somewhere. And if the judge thinks I've got the authority, I'll make it the same across the street in front of the hardware store."

Youngblood left shortly afterward to get a little sleep, since he was to be awakened about two o'clock in the morning. Maggie cornered him out of earshot of the sheriff, still wrought up by the escape, and said, "Mr. Youngblood, I sure am sorry. Mr. Ivey told me he just wanted him a little exercise. That's what he told me: he only wanted him some exercise."

"He got some," the deputy told her. He started to tell her not to worry about it, but reconsidered; the sheriff would tell her it was all right as soon as he had calmed down.

The following day both the sheriff and Youngblood were in the office when Ogle sent the message by a hotel porter. He wanted to see the sheriff. He would appreciate if the sheriff would come to his room at the hotel.

"I guess he would," the sheriff told the man. "You tell Ogle he knows where he can find me. I got no business with him but public business, and I got an office where I do public business. If he wants to see me, he can come down here."

An hour later Ogle appeared. Youngblood had noted at the Cattlemen's Association meeting two weeks earlier that the man did not seem to actually be a leader of the ranchers, but more like their tool. In his hesitancy and uncertainty it seemed as if he were a front, chosen because he would do as someone else wanted him to do. Today he did not seem happy with his visit to the sheriff's office.

"Sheriff Bell, I felt I ought to . . ." he began. "Or, that is, I represent a group of men that felt I ought to . . ."

The sheriff interrupted, "What group of men?"

"A group of . . . well, cattlemen."

"You speaking for the Cattlemen's Association?" The sheriff evidently was not too happy about the visit either, had judged the old man somewhat as had Youngblood, and did not intend to make it easy for him.

"No, but I speak for this group . . . uh, an unofficial group, you might say."

"Why don't you speak for yourself, and let them speak for theirselves?"

"Well, I've just agreed to speak for the group," Ogle went on, doggedly, though flustered. "There's a feeling something ought to be done about this possible violence."

"What in the Sam Hill are you talking about?" the sheriff asked. "Violence? Do you know anything about any violence, Youngblood? Ain't nobody started cutting fences again, have they?"

"No sir," the deputy said. "Everything seems pretty quiet to me."

"Maybe you mean about hanging William Ivey," the sheriff said. "We do aim to hang him, and I guess he would think it's kind of violent."

Ogle's face flushed. "I think you understand what I mean, Sheriff Bell. Some of the . . . uh, group . . . they don't intend to see Ivey hang. I'm one who thinks some kind of compromise might be best for everybody. Perhaps Ivey might be fined or perhaps sent to prison for a period . . . uh . . ."

"Why shouldn't he be hung, like he was sentenced?"

"Because . . . well, certain men will not allow it. Some people may get killed, and all respect for the law will be destroyed. Surely this can be prevented by some kind of compromise."

"Ogle, are you saying you aim to try to break Ivey out?"

"No, I didn't say that. I . . . uh . . . don't say that I would condone anything illegal, but . . ."

"Then why don't you shut up about it. I'm getting pretty stinking tired of fellers that sneak around and make threats and act lily white and honest and upstanding. All I've heard for two weeks is that the sheriff and his men better stick their tail between their legs and run, because they're fixing to take a beating. Who's going to

100

do it? Let them show their face. If you ain't going to do anything illegal, then don't come around here threatening, and you better stop carrying messages for fellers that are afraid to show their own face."

Ogle was thoroughly confused by the sheriff's tirade. He started to speak twice, seriously concerned with the failure of his mission, then gave up, but at the door got out the words "When . . . When they show their faces, it'll be too late."

The sheriff had made his arrangements at the blacksmith shop. After Slim came in from his morning rounds, all four of the lawmen took Ivey out and put him in a wagon and took him to the other end of town. The wagon was for return transportation; the prisoner wouldn't be able to walk.

From the time he left his cell, all the way down main street, Ivey tried to talk the sheriff out of it. He promised everything he could think of. At the front of the barn-like blacksmith shop, he began to curse. The sheriff still would not answer him, except to say, "Get down."

Ivey rose, but suddenly shouted "Hyah! Git!" at the team and clapped his hands. Youngblood jumped in front of the mules and grabbed their bridles. Andy and Slim scrambled back into the wagon. The sheriff, who had been almost jerked off his feet, said, "That was smart! You damned fool, it looks like you're trying to make everything just as rough on yourself as you can. Now, how do you want it, boy? I believe us four and old Eb can put them irons on you. Do you want us to do it with you conscious or unconscious? If we have to knock you out, don't blame anybody but yourself if they don't fit. Just make up your mind."

The three in the wagon hustled Ivey out, one on each arm and one behind. The sheriff had been serious about his threat, or thought he had, but was never able to bring himself to knock the man out. Ivey fought all the way, so that they found it necessary to stretch him out flat in the dirt floor among the dried horse manure while old Eb fitted the shackles to his ankles. They were two hinged circles of heavy strap iron held together with four links of log chain.

Two boys, some eight years old, came and stood in the open front doorway of the shop to watch, wide eyed.

101

When the sheriff noticed them, he shooed them away brusquely.

The blacksmith was a powerful old man with a mangy-looking beard. When he cranked at his forge or calmly pounded red iron on his anvil, he would forget that anyone was present and would sing mournfully,

"I got a gal on Sourwood Mountain
Hey my day. My diddle-dum day.
Get your hat and we'll go a courting.
Hey my day. My diddle-dum day.

He would pound the shackles around the point of his anvil, cool them in a barrel of water, and try them. Ivey cursed and kicked. "I've forged these things before," Eb said, "but I don't believe I ever seen a man so set agin wearing them." When he had shaped them to his own satisfaction, he pinned each side solid with a half-inch rivit.

"Get up," the sheriff said.

Ivey lay still. "I can't get up, and I ain't going to wear these God-damned chains. I ain't no slave."

They picked him up and carried him out and dumped him into the wagon bed as if he were a towsack of potatoes. Word about it had gone through town. Storekeepers came out on their front porches and here and there a human figure hung out of a second-storey window, watching the sheriff's department haul their shackled prisoner back to jail.

He pounded and yelled in his cell, even found a way to strike one ankle iron against the steel bars, but by afternoon he had stopped. Youngblood, sitting alone in the sheriff's office, was glad for the quiet. He didn't mind the noise but had found himself thinking, "He sure makes it hard on himself." He had a pity for the man, not like Maggie, the cook, but more like someone who sees a rattlesnake being stoned.

Voices sounded in argument out in front of the building. Youngblood stepped to the door and saw it was Judge Pendergrass and the dude lawyer who had stayed in Comanche Wells. The deputy stepped back in order not to appear to be eavesdropping, but they spoke loudly and stopped in front of the door so that he couldn't help but hear.

"You can't do a thing to change the outcome," the judge was saying. "Not that I know of, but that doesn't remove all your responsibility from an ethical standpoint. It doesn't mean you ought to catch a stage and hightail it out of here without saying anything to anybody."

"But, Your Honor, I fear for my life."

"Don't 'Your Honor' me. We're not in court and this isn't a legal matter; it's a matter of common decency. I fear for my life too. This is the least you can do: inform those who have paid your fee and also your client about the developments and tell them that you are resigning from the case. You might do more: some lawyers might feel they had a duty to the people who had hired them, these men you say you fear, to persuade them against violence."

"But you said yourself, Judge Pendergrass, violence seems more natural to them than legal methods, and I have discovered that you are surely right. I'm not going back to one of their meetings again; they'll lynch me."

"All right then, Counselor, let me suggest this: some lawyers might think they had an obligation to their client, to stick by him. Do you know the man's in irons right now? Do you care? Now the sheriff has a right to use whatever methods he thinks necessary to keep the man in custody, but I think it's only common decency to stick by him and let him know that somebody is concerned for his comfort."

"My colleagues got out of the situation," the lawyer said bitterly.

"So that's all you can think of—to get out of the situation," the judge said. "Well, at least you are going to notify your employers and your client. Mr. Ogle, the president of the Cattlemen's Association, is in town; I presume you are not afraid to tell him. He'll find out through rumor anyway. Come in."

The judge urged the lawyer into the office without touching him, through sheer will power. "Mr. Youngblood," the judge said, "we would like to see the prisoner, William Ivey."

The deputy led them upstairs to the cell. Ivey lay on his bunk. The lawyer stood in front of the bars, the judge behind him, and recited, like an unwilling school boy giving a reading, "I am sorry to inform you, Mr.

Ivey, that your appeal has been denied. I can do no more for you and am resigning from your case."

Ivey said savagely, "Why you smooth-talking, pale-face, lily-livered son-of-a-bitch! Get me out of here! Get this damn iron off my legs!"

As the dude lawyer went down the stairs and out of the building, his face was as pale as death.

Chapter 12

EDITOR EZRA PITTS came out of the front door of his establishment, his usual dirty apron on and his white shirt spotted with printers' ink. Youngblood nodded at him and was about to pass on.

"Oh, Mr. Youngblood, wait," the editor said. "Could you give me a minute of your time?"

"Well, I suppose one minute," the deputy said, laughing. "What can I do for you?"

"Well, you helped me before. In fact, you gave me some excellent advice about an editorial, the day before Ivey was convicted, you remember? Now I was wondering if you would look at another one. Maybe you could tell me something that would help me. As you know, I'm rather new to this part of the country, but I'm determined to learn the customs, you might say, and build up respect for the free press."

"I'm afraid I don't know much about newspaper work, Mr. Pitts."

"But I'm asking you as an expert on the subject matter," the editor said. "It's about the Rangers who are coming here."

"I'm sure enough afraid you've got the wrong man," Youngblood laughed. "In fact, nobody at the sheriff's department knows much that's definite. A feller named Lieutenant Ruth has been assigned to bring a detachment out here, but we've got no idea when they'll come or how many men. In fact, they don't know in Austin; they're just going to pull a few men off of other duties."

"I know that, Mr. Youngblood; I know that. But, you

see, this is an editorial. You don't need the facts to write an editorial. Come in. Let me show you. You see, the press has a responsibility to throw its weight behind issues by stating its position."

The strip of proof he handed Youngblood read thus:

"!Warning to Apostles of Violence!
An Editorial Concerning the Preservation of Our Priceless Heritage, Law and Order

"We are highly Gratified to Bring editorial comment once more in the case of the Infamous Killer William Ivey, who now reposes in the Local Carroll County jail, convicted of a Dastardly Murder.

"Men of Good Will will greet with pleasure the Recent news that a Considerable force of Gallant Texas Rangers are to be assigned to Comanche Wells in the Near Future. This troop will be under the command of Lieutenant Ruth, an Experienced and Efficient officer, who, it is assumed, will Brook no Interference in the performance of his Duties. Let those who plan unlawful Acts Beware.

"What is the Purpose of the Gallant Lawmen in coming to our fair City at this time? To Guarantee that the legal sentence given William Ivey be executed, namely Hanged By The Neck Until Dead. That the good people of this Region Co-operate fully with both Rangers and our Local Sheriff is, in the words of the Immortal Bard, "A consumation Devoutly to be Wished."

"One citizen has made an Informed estimate as to the number of Rangers to be Stationed here during our Time of Need, and he states that probably Forty (40) Rangers may be Expected, since that is the Number which might Properly be Commanded by a Lieutenant. Lawless Elements, which according to generally Reliable Sources, plan to break Ivey Free and thus Thwart the Law, should take Cognizance of these Facts, lest our local Prison be Filled with Additional Lawbreakers."

105

Editor Pitts stood waiting expectantly. "Well, what do you think, Mr. Youngblood?"

The deputy scratched his head and grinned. "I'm afraid I never would make a newspaper man, Mr. Pitts."

"Why not?"

"I just can't seem to get used to all that fancy language."

"Well, now, it does take considerable practice to master the language, Mr. Youngblood. One of my hopes in coming to this part of the country is that I may be able, in a small way, to bring appreciation of good writing and other cultural attainments. Have you noticed the original poems I've been running?"

"Yes sir, they're fine," Youngblood said. "I was wondering where you got that number 'forty' in the editorial, Mr. Pitts."

"An editor never divulges the source of his information. Why do you wonder?"

"I just thought it sounded like a pretty wild guess."

"Well, I'll tell you a little trade secret, Mr. Youngblood, if you'll promise never to divulge it: I made it up. I am the 'citizen' referred to. I thought it was a good round number, a reasonable number. Do you think it will be more or less?"

The deputy thought it would be considerably less, but he told the editor, "I appreciate your confidence in me, Mr. Pitts, but I honestly don't have any information, and as far as opinion goes, I wish you would ask the sheriff." He laughed. "The sheriff is as dumb as I am about fine writing, but he has more official opinions."

He left thinking that it probably didn't make any difference what the *Courier* printed. The rumor about the Rangers was over town, and you could hear almost any version you wanted to. Anyway, he would report Pitts' coming editorial to his superior.

As he passed the Robert Lee Hotel, he was stopped in a less friendly manner by a second man, who did not ask him for a minute of his time.

"Hey, you! Star-toter!" It was the rancher Bledsoe.

The deputy stopped and eyed him without answering. The rancher was a heavy man, slightly chubby but powerful, with a red complexion. He reminded the deputy of the cowhand of old man Long he had been in the fist fight with.

"I was headed for the sheriff's office," Bledsoe said, "but I reckon you'll do."

"Yeah? Do for what?"

"To soak up a little information, Star-toter. I'll make it real simple so you or the sheriff either one can understand it. That spy of yours is fixing to get himself killed."

Youngblood was trying his best to make some sense out of the words. Finally he said, "I don't know what you're talking about."

"You know what I'm talking about, all right. That damned greaser Torres. We know he's working for the sheriff, but he ain't going to be working for anybody if he comes on my ranch again, and that goes for most of the ranchers around here. He's been spying around our meetings twice that we know of, and we nearly caught him last night. Next time, it's going to be the end of him."

The deputy was trying to make it add up and also trying to get all the information he could. He asked, "How do you know it was Torres?"

"Don't worry about that. We know him when we see him. We've seen him around town here enough. Some of you two-bit lawmen are going to learn that we cattlemen ain't as stupid as you think. You're not fooling anybody yourself, Youngblood. You're trying to make Mr. Pendergrass think you might come over to the ranchers, but you wouldn't leave that precious sheriff, and we know it. You haven't got Mr. Pendergrass fooled a bit.

"You haven't got anybody fooled on this damned greaser either. You call him off, or he's going to get shot. Seems like you high-and-mighty lawmen have got the idea you can play the game any way you want, and you don't have to obey the law yourself. Well, you got to have a search warrant to come on my place, or you're liable to get shot for a prowler and a trespasser. And that's exactly what that damned greaser's going to get next time you send him out there to spy."

"That all you got to say?" Youngblood asked.

They glared at each other a moment, then each turned and walked away. The deputy headed for the courthouse.

What they had suspected about Torres now seemed

107

certain. The ranchers honestly didn't know him. Stephen Pendergrass had taken the man for a bank robber, and now Bledsoe had taken him for a spy working for the sheriff. This could only mean one thing: the Mexican's loyalty to Ivey went back to the time before Ivey came to Comanche Wells, probably to the days of cavalry scouting since they spoke the same Indian dialect. And Torres was doing some private investigation, entirely on his own; maybe he had not had time to discover in his interview with Ivey the identity of the unknown party who had employed the gunman, and now he was trying to find out by spying. Or maybe he knew the identity and sought to make sure that the unknown party paid his debt to Ivey by breaking him out.

Both the sheriff and the judge agreed with Youngblood's speculation about the Mexican as they discussed Bledsoe's threats, and they agreed that Torres would bear watching, though it was not likely he would attempt a jailbreak by himself. At least, the judge pointed out, the Mexican had the ranchers confused.

This was the day that Charlie Moss came back to town and came down to the jail to inform Youngblood that his wife was home again. The deputy waited impatiently for the hour when he could go off duty, supposedly to sleep; then he headed home. The eleven days since he had seen his wife seemed six months; her silent tears when he left her at the ranch had never been far out of his mind. He was glad that he had made it home two days before to open the windows and air out the house, also to water what remained of Lila's cantaloupe vines.

His Aunt Annie met him at the door and told him that Lila was in the garden. She stood still and waited for him to come to her, as if she were in no hurry, but the way she clung to him for a minute gave the lie to it; and he remembered how he had scolded her for waiting up for him and running to him, like a fiest, he had said.

She was bigger, he thought, and clumsier, not emotional but innocently gay. She was obviously pleased at coming back to their home and to him. Of her trip to the Moss ranch and her letter begging to come back, she said nothing directly, only some light kidding words in the knowledge that he would know what she was talking about: "I guess after I'm all well again, I get a good spanking, don't I?"

"A spanking?" he asked in mock disdain. "You get a good cow-hiding!"

"What's a cow-hiding?"

"You'll find out."

"It sounds interesting and kind of bad too."

"It's worse than that," he told her. "It's horrible."

She did not seem disappointed that he had to go back to the jail to sleep. Youngblood sensed that she was able to draw a kind of strength from his aunt. The older woman was calm and methodical. When he asked if he could go carry groceries or anything before he had to leave, his Aunt Annie said, "No, you go get to bed. I can carry groceries, and Lila will go with me; walking is good for her."

He kissed his wife, without saying when he might come back, and left.

Chapter 13

DEPUTY YOUNGBLOOD thought to himself that he would take the irons off, if it were his decision. Ivey had hardly had an easy minute since the heavy rivets were set. The deputy pushed the dinner tray under the cell door. Ivey had been alternating between periods of violent struggling and sullen silence; now he seemed to be in one of his silent periods as he stood gripping the bars.

As the deputy was turning away, Ivey's chain clanked and his bare foot struck the tray, sending it clattering out into the corridor. The tin cup, which had been full of coffee, rolled away. Maggie's beans were strewed across the floor. The prisoner continued to stare in silent contempt at the deputy.

Youngblood stared back at him for a minute. "Ivey, I don't understand you," he said. "You gripe about being mistreated but you bring it all on yourself. You've got ten days to go, feller. Can't you see you're just making it harder on yourself."

Ivey continued to stare.

"Now I've got to clean up this mess," Youngblood said. "Do you think that's going to make me want to see you treated better?"

"Why don't you send that old bitch Maggie to clean it up?"

" 'That old bitch Maggie,' as you call her, is about the only friend you've got around here, feller. I don't know why you call her names. And you know the sheriff won't let her up here, and I wouldn't either."

Youngblood went downstairs to get some equipment to use in the cleaning job. When the sheriff heard about the incident, he said that Ivey was not to have any food until supper. The deputy went back upstairs with broom, dustpan, mop, and mop bucket. Ivey was still standing in the same place.

"I guess you'll be yelling that we're starving you," Youngblood said. "The sheriff says this was all the grub you get till supper."

"To hell with the sheriff and his grub. What do I care about grub? I got to get these irons off; I can't stand them. It ain't human."

"You mean you don't like to stand them," Youngblood said, swishing the wet mop across the wooden floor.

"What the hell do you know about what I mean? You ever wear any irons?"

"No, and I hope I never have to. I never shot any kids either."

"Well, you don't know what it's like. I already got sores on my ankles. I can't stand it. I got to move around a little."

Youngblood said quietly as he started to go back downstairs, "If you didn't kick around so much, you wouldn't hurt your ankles."

"Wait, Youngblood. I want you to get the sheriff up here. I'm ready to make a deal. I'll confess."

The deputy went down and told the sheriff. "You reckon he means it?" the sheriff asked, interested.

"He means something. He says he can't stand those irons, and you can tell he means it."

"Go get the judge. We'll find out."

Youngblood found Judge Pendergrass in his office and

brought him back, and the three of them went upstairs to confront Ivey. The prisoner was sitting on his bunk with his elbows on his knees.

"All right, Ivey, make your deal," the sheriff said.

"You take these damn irons off, and I'll confess."

"What do you mean—'confess'? Confess to what?"

"Hell, if I told you that, you wouldn't have no reason to make a deal then. Take these damn irons off and I'll tell you."

The sheriff folded his heavy arms and paused a moment, then said, "Ivey, I'm not too sure I've got any reason to make a deal with you anyway. You're the one that wanted to make a deal. And I'll tell you for derned sure I'm not going to take the irons off first. I wouldn't take them off till after you get through talking."

"Will you give me your word to take them off if I confess?"

The judge interrupted, "Sheriff, I think maybe what you want to do is specify that he must tell you a certain man's name."

The sheriff turned back to the prisoner. "You heard it, Ivey. You've got my word on the leg irons, if you'll tell us the man that paid you and give us some dope to help convict him."

"I can't do that."

"Why can't you?"

"Well, it might cost me my life. But I'll tell you some things you don't know."

The sheriff laughed, more as a matter of putting on a front in the dickering than from mirth. "Cost you your life? What's it worth? You haven't got much over a week left."

"I'll tell you some things you don't know," Ivey insisted.

The sheriff looked at the judge and the judge shrugged. Finally the sheriff said, "All right, feller, if you won't make any deal, I won't either. If you want to talk, go ahead. If you tell us enough that we really want to know, the irons come off. That's as far as I'll go."

Ivey moistened his lips with his tongue and talked. "I killed the damned sheepherder's kid. But it was a mistake; I thought it was Munson. I never killed anybody on purpose but what had it coming to them. The damned

111

kid had on a big jumper and a hat like his old man wore." Ivey spoke without any emotion.

"Go on," the sheriff said.

"That's all they was to it. I was laying up on the rock where you found the hulls when he come out of the creek bottom. I let him have it, and he raised up and went dragging off, so I let him have it again. But I never knowed it was the kid till I turned him over."

"How much were you paid to kill Munson?"

"I wasn't paid at all. I was going to do it on my own."

"Why?"

"Because he cussed me. I rode by his place and he cussed me good. I don't have to take that off of a damned sheepherder."

"Go on."

"That's all they was to it."

"Well, Ivey, I don't see where you think you've told us much. You been found guilty of killing the kid whether you ever confessed it or not. Hell, you ought to of confessed it just to ease your conscience."

The judge broke the ensuing silence with a question. "Who is this fellow Torres?"

"He used to be a buddy of mine," Ivey said. "Name's Juan, Juan Torres."

The sheriff took up the questioning again. "Is he working with the ranchers?"

"No."

"How do you know?"

"Well, I mean I don't think so. Juan don't take to strangers much, and he don't know anybody around here."

"Is he working for the same feller that paid you?"

"No."

"Is he hanging around here to help you some way?"

"I don't know. He would help me if he could. He used to be a good buddy of mine."

The sheriff stood in silence for a minute, then motioned with his head, and the judge and Youngblood followed him to the end of the corridor where their voices would not be heard by the prisoner.

"What do you think?" the sheriff asked the judge.

"I think he's told the truth so far."

Youngblood said, "You know I told you about seeing

112

Munson out there that day. His story about the cussing was the same as Ivey's."

The sheriff scratched his head. "Shoot, I don't know. Even if he's told the truth, he hasn't told us any too much we hadn't already guessed. The thing is, he can't ride to do any good the way he is, if they broke him out. And if they took him out of here like he is, they would have to stop somewhere pretty soon to get the irons off, maybe a half hour it would cost them." He paused as if for any suggestions. The judge said nothing. The sheriff asked Youngblood, "What do you think? I imagine you've got some opinions on it, since he jumped you the other day."

Youngblood grinned. "I guess if it was up to me I would take them off. He doesn't deserve good treatment, but it seems like it hurts him more to be tied up than it would most people."

The sheriff asked the judge, "I don't guess you've got any word on the big detachment of Rangers that fool editor Pitts writes about in his paper?"

"Nothing definite. I think they ought to be here by the week end."

The sheriff turned suddenly and said, "Hell, we'll take them off. We ought to be able to hold a man inside a jail without irons on his legs." He went over in front of the cell and shook his big, stubby finger at the prisoner, who was still sitting on the bunk. "All right, Ivey, I'm going to get the blacksmith up here and see if he can chisel those things off. Now you listen to me and you listen good—you got them put on you because you tried to escape. You try anything again and I'm going to hogtie you up to where you can't hardly bat your eyes. You just try me and see."

Youngblood went downtown to find old Eb, the blacksmith. After leaving a message for him, he came back and met Slim in front of McSween's Saloon. "You won't have to listen to Ivey pounding tonight," he told the skinny deputy.

"What happened? The sheriff lose his patience and beat him to death?"

Youngblood told him about the confession and the deal to take the irons off. Slim shook his head and said, "I

113

ain't too sure it's a good time to take his irons off. I been hearing all kinds of rumors around town today."

"Such as what?"

"Well, screwy things, you know. Like the cattlemen are going to flood the jail, a bunch of them got in jail on purpose. And like a mob of people here in town are going to break Ivey out and lynch him."

"Who's talking about the lynching?"

"Hell, I've heard it a dozen places. They won't talk much around me. You know, they just say they *heard* about it. But old man Wiley is one that's in favor of it."

Slim had to go out to the *Cantina,* and Youngblood went back to the courthouse to pass the rumors on to the sheriff and the judge, who was still in the sheriff's office. The judge was concerned. The man Wiley, whom Slim had mentioned, was a county commissioner who owned a dryland farm, which was worked by his son, and owned the Alamo Groceries and Provisions Co., which he ran himself.

"Judge," the sheriff said, "we've got a chance to get around some of this trouble, and I'd like to know how you see it. You could move up the date. That lazy Cobb ought to finish the scaffold today. What's to keep us from swinging Ivey at sunrise tomorrow?"

The judge was thoughtful. "It's the same question as taking him to Briggsburg or hanging him inside. The way I see it, if they break Ivey out and he gets away, we lose. But if you take a gun upstairs right now and shoot him dead, we lose too. We don't really completely win unless we hang him right out there in the open on August the first. Personally, I'd hate to compromise a bit more than we have to. What do you think? Have you begun to doubt that we can hold him?"

"I don't know. We don't know what we can count on from the Rangers, and we don't know what we'll get from these blooming people in town. What do you think? You know as much about it as I do."

"I'll make a deal with you," the Judge said, smiling. "If you decide we can't hold him, you let me know, and I'll move the date; and if I decide we can't hold him, I'll let you know. In the meantime, we've got to straighten out people like Wiley. He's an elected county official. How do you stand with your town posse?"

"I've got a list of a dozen men I think will take orders.

114

I don't know what they'll do in a fight. I've talked to all of them."

"I believe I'd go ahead and swear them in," the judge said. "Is Wiley on your list?"

"No. Like we was saying before, Judge, we got to have men on the posse that will follow orders. We're going to have a mess if we don't. And Wiley is kind of stubborn. You figure he ought to be on it?"

"It might help to put down this talk about lynching."

"Would you want to talk to him? I can't talk to a stubborn man like that, Judge, to do any good."

"Sure, if you'd like for me to."

The sheriff turned to Youngblood. "Get Wiley in here."

He went down to the big barn-like building of the Alamo Groceries and Provisions Co. and found the man out back helping to load a wagon full of cedar posts and barbed wire. Wiley was a fat man, and now the old army grays he wore were spotted darkly with sweat. He seemed relieved at an excuse to stop and talk and leave the heavy work to his clerk. The deputy told him vaguely that he was wanted on some kind of county business.

The judge and the sheriff solemnly shook hands with the man in the sheriff's office and offered him a chair.

"Mr. Wiley," the judge said, "I've been talking with the sheriff about some of his problems, and we thought it would be a good idea to consult with you since you are a county official and also a landowner and also a leading citizen among the townspeople here. It has occurred to us that you have a rather broad understanding of the problems of this area."

The fat man smiled. "Well, sometimes I think I've got a little influence; sometimes I ain't so sure."

"Well," the judge went on, "I was assuring the sheriff that we stand behind him in this Ivey trouble. I mean the elected officials as well as the influential citizens such as yourself."

The fat man crossed his legs. "Well, what I think about the Ivey trouble is if the sheriff was to turn his head, there would be some people in town that would take care of him, if you know what I mean. The people in town ain't fighting people like the ranchers, but they can't be pushed but only so far."

"I knew that you would be concerned about that," the judge said. "I believe you are thinking along the same

115

lines as the sheriff and myself to some extent. Our primary problem, of course, is to execute the sentence exactly according to law, and we feel that even though the townspeople are not fighting people, as you have pointed out, that they are certainly not weaklings and that they will uphold the law and the dignity of our government at every level. And as I say, I was assuring the sheriff that he can count on us who are elected officials and some who, such as yourself, are also of influence in the community to help the citizens of the county to realize that the mistake the ranchers are making lies in not being willing to abide by the law. Of course, as you realize, our job is not to *kill* Ivey, but to make sure that the sentence of our court is carried out; and we realize that some people don't understand what we mean by that; we mean that he must be hanged exactly according to the law, in spite of any opposition from anyone whether he be a cattleman or a person with a business in town. But as I said, you understand these matters because you are a landowner as well as a man of importance in other ways, and I think I can say to the sheriff that you are a man who will help explain this to other people such as your customers.

"But one of the sheriff's problems that we wanted to get your help on is the matter of a special posse to stand by and be ready to help if needed. The sheriff is concerned about getting people signed up and sworn in who will follow instructions exactly. These people are not fighting people, but they can't be pushed too far, as you have pointed out. They have a solid strength underneath and a desire to see that the law is followed to the letter. But, of course, since they have had no training in the work of a lawman it is extremely important that they follow instructions exactly, so that the dignity of the law is maintained. Perhaps you have some suggestions, Mr. Wiley. We would like your opinion. How can we be sure that our posse members will do exactly as they are instructed by our elected law officials?"

The fat man blinked his small eyes and crossed his legs the other way. "They would just have to be told, that's all. I think they would just have to be told. And they would have to follow instructions."

"I think that is an excellent suggestion," the judge said. "The people will rise to the occasion if they are told,

116

especially if they are told by leaders who are from their own ranks and yet have influence. I can see that you and I and the sheriff are thinking along the same lines. Now, I have told the sheriff that I will help in any way I can. How about you, Mr. Wiley, can the sheriff put you down as a member of the special posse? We seriously need men of your caliber."

"Well, I'd help any way I could. Course, I got my store to run. What would I have to do?"

"The main thing a posse member will need to do is provide himself with a saddle horse and a gun and stand ready for the sheriff's call, day or night, during the next week. Of course, the sheriff might be able to help with the horse or the gun."

"I don't ride much any more," the fat man said.

"Well, actually, Mr. Wiley, I think you would be more valuable as a sort of honorary member of the posse. I mean that you can use your influence with the other people in town and help explain to them how necessary it is to follow legal processes and follow the instructions of the sheriff."

"Put me down," Mr. Wiley said to the sheriff. "I aim to do my duty. When will that big bunch of Rangers be here?"

"I'm glad you brought that up," the judge told him. "I think some of the people in town may be disappointed. Of course, you and I realize, Mr. Wiley, that we're not going to get forty Rangers out here just because trouble is threatened. We don't care if some of the cattlemen who intend to make trouble hold a mistaken idea, but the townspeople should be told that we can't expect that many Rangers. If disregard for the law were flaunted in Carroll County and Ivey were broken free and several lawmen were killed, then the Rangers would be sent here in great force. But for a threat, no.

"Of course, our main problem is to convince the townspeople, Mr. Wiley, that we can handle the job ourselves. The good citizens of this county have convicted Ivey and sentenced him, and now I'm sure that they are not going to back down; as you say, they can be pushed only so far."

The fat man was nodding or shaking his head according to the words of the judge. He finally rose to leave and the judge followed him out, still talking. Youngblood laughed and the sheriff laughed and said, "If I could talk

117

like that damn little old judge, I would run for the governor of this state."

About noon on July 27th, the Ranger detachment arrived—four men. They came in by the south road and made their way the length of main street, sitting their long-legged horses easily, looking at the town. They were not on parade, but rather rode in an informal bunch, like men who have been on serious missions together; an observer could not tell which one was the leader. Behind them they pulled two haltered pack horses with neatly tied loads.

The townspeople who noticed them shook their heads and muttered, "Only four?" But when the bunch pulled up at the jail, the sheriff came out and greeted them warmly and said nothing about how few they were.

Chapter 14

IT WAS July 30th. Deputy Youngblood was in charge of the station on the south road a half mile out of town. For help he had the Ranger they called Smitty and two special possemen, old Eb and a young dry-goods clerk.

The road was ungraded, only two shallow ruts in the sparse grass. Here where the ground sloped down toward Seedy Creek the ruts had washed out in places and detours had been worn out to either side so that the location of the road was anybody's choice. Youngblood had looked over the ground carefully when they came out at daybreak. He had chosen the spot here by the willows because they would not be too obvious to anyone coming toward town, yet would not be concealed; it did not look like an ambush. Their horses were tied in the creek bottom.

He had stationed Smitty with his rifle two hundred feet back from the road, near enough to see clearly but a long distance for a hand gun. The Ranger had thought it a good idea and was sitting on the ground now with his back against a live oak tree, his rifle lying carelessly across his legs, pointed toward where they waited by the willow clump.

Youngblood had chosen the Ranger for the rifle post because he didn't trust either of the others to use good judgment at such a distance. Old Eb was calmly chewing tobacco and moaning snatches of "Sourwood Mountain," not concerned that drops of amber juice stained his mangy beard. He looked as if he might be able to use the shotgun he carried, but the young drygoods clerk had appeared pale and nervous since he had strapped on the new pearl-handled .45. The two had definite instructions not to fire unless fired upon. As for the use of his own gun, the deputy had orders which did not exactly please him even though he agreed with them. The sheriff and Lieutenant Ruth had felt that none of them could afford to act like gentlemen. The orders of the sheriff had been, "Don't wait for none of these rannies to draw on you. Do your talking with your gun in your hand."

Youngblood had been watching the two approaching cowboys a couple of minutes before they saw him. They drew up their trotting horses, looking uncertain, then apparently talked about it. Then they came on, letting their horses walk and pick their way among the ruts of the old road down the gentle slope.

They did not call out but approached warily as if to pass without any words. Youngblood let them get as near as the distance across a room before he stepped into the road, bringing up his gun quickly. "Hold it, fellers!"

One of them said, "What's going on here?" and the other, "What's the matter?"

Youngblood had thumbed the hammer back on his .44. "Keep your hands where I can see them," he said. Seeing that they made no aggressive move, he tilted the barrel of his gun away from them. "Fellers, we got a new rule in town. For the next three days, no guns. You'll have to take those off here or turn around and ride back where you came from."

They were two tough looking riders. The skinny one said, "Hell, I don't care nothing about your town rules. I ain't going to take off my guns."

"Then you won't go into town," the deputy told him.

The other cowboy said, "What's that blacksmith and that damn dude there doing? They're wearing guns."

119

"They're both deputies. Sworn in by the sheriff."

"I never heard such bull in all my life," the skinny one said. "This is a nervous horse I'm riding, star-toter. If I sink these spurs in his flanks, he'll run right over you."

"You try that," Youngblood said. He moved his gun back to cover the skinny one and invited again, "Come on. Spur him."

The man was tense. His left hand held the reins and his right was clenched near the saddle horn about twelve inches from his gun. He was almost ready to try it.

"That *hombre* back over yonder by that tree is a Ranger," Youngblood said quietly. "He's a crack shot with that rifle he's got pointed this way. Did you ever hear that rumor about Rangers? That they get a bonus for every man they kill in the line of duty?"

The skinny man let his clenched hand open and rest on the saddle horn. The other cowboy said, "Look, Deputy, we work for old man Underwood. He told us to meet him in town, and you know how strict he is. Let us go on in and meet him and we'll tell him what you said about checking our guns. We got to take orders from him."

"Why, feller, I don't care who you meet or who you take orders from," the deputy said. "But you got just two choices right now: hand down your guns, or else turn around and go back."

They sat without speaking for a half minute and Youngblood could almost see the working of the mind of the skinny one; he was thinking about their chances of getting through; then he decided that they could not. He reined around slowly, careful not to start anything. The other cowboy followed him, and they rode back south.

The deputy and the two townsmen stood in the road and watched them disappear. The drygoods clerk began to chatter about this and that, saying little. The day was becoming warm. Youngblood called the Ranger over and told him, "They said they were going to meet Mr. Underwood in town, but I don't think Mr. Underwood is in town now. I'm going to ride up on the ridge and look around a little. I would like for you fellers to stick pretty close here."

He took the big bay gelding out of the creek bottom and rode up the gentle rise toward the south, not along the road but angling toward the west where the ridge was higher. He sat his horse on the high ground and lengthened his grip on the reins so the animal could crop at the bunch grass. Behind him he could see all of Comanche Wells, from the scattered adobes on this side to the courthouse and the high ground around it.

He tried to locate his own house among the hazy mixture of rooftops but could not and it bothered him a little. Somewhere there Lila was waiting. He wondered what she was doing and what she was thinking. The fleeting idea that she might already be in labor crossed his mind and he pushed it back.

It's July 30th, he thought. And tomorrow is the 31st, and the next is August 1st. The next two days loomed as big as years. Funny, how days rolled along, got away from you, passed without thought of their passing; then two of them, only two, loomed up like violent years to be dealt with.

The vision of his father in the new gray uniform came to him. It didn't mean what it had once meant. He was even beginning to see that no man could possibly have been what he had thought his father was. The thing that intrigued him was that he had seen no hint of the coming tragedy in the uniform or the going away. Why hadn't his mother cried? But of course the truth was that she had cried, without doubt, and had hidden her tears, and a boy doesn't search for a hint of tragedy.

It was all a bunch of damned foolishness, relating his father to his situation today. The thing didn't seem to apply to himself, anyway, but to Lila. And he wasn't any kind of blind kid today. She was a healthy woman and would bear a strong child, and he was a sentimental fool. Again he pushed her from his mind.

Out to the south he could see nothing across the gently rolling plains. Over to the west, a half mile, was the southwest corner of the fenced portion of the big Rail-P. Cattle were strung out; he could see some as far as two miles away, like ants, red spots against the half-dry grass. They were all pointed the same way, grazing toward a windmill which was barely visible against the horizon. He could see it because he knew what it looked like with

121

its darker soil around it, dampened by the leaking from the troughs, trampled free of grass by sharp cattle hooves, spotted by dark droppings.

When his eyes swung south again, he saw the riders. He pulled up his horse's head and put his right hand up to shield his eyes. There were five of them. He could not make out anything else, except that they were men accustomed to the saddle. He would have bet that two of them were the two they had already turned back, and another was probably Underwood. At their pace, it would be ten minutes.

He rode back down into the creek and tied the bay among the other horses, then walked back up to the willow clump. "We've got some more visitors coming, fellers. Five this time. They may figure there's enough of them to bull their way through."

"You want me the same place?" Smitty asked.

"Yeah, unless you've got a better idea. And say, Smitty, I want to be real sure we understand each other. If I heard the sheriff and the lieutenant right, they mean for us to stop these cowboys or get their guns. It's not any bluff on our part at all."

"We're right together, me and you," the Ranger said, grinning. "In fact, we got a kind of a policy, Youngblood; don't draw your gun unless you're ready to use it. If the bunch gets by you, I'll guarantee to lay down two or three of them before they get in the creek."

"Say we draw a line about right here," Youngblood said, swinging his hand across the road. "Right across here. Eb, that's a real dangerous gun you've got there at close range. Keep it on them but don't get trigger happy."

To the drygoods clerk he said, "That .45 will buck pretty bad with you if you're not used to firing it. I'd like you to fire at the horse instead of the man. But let's don't fire at all unless they start it or cross our line."

The riders had come close enough so that they could be identified. Underwood was in the lead and Ogle in the rear. The skinny man and his partner were with them, and probably the other cowboy was one of Ogle's hands. Underwood drew up forty feet from them and said in his womanish voice, which was a contrast to his stern face, "Let's stop this blamed foolishness, Deputy. Get out of the road!"

Youngblood had his gun centered on the old man's

122

chest. "As you have heard, Mr. Underwood, we have a new rule in town: no guns today or tomorrow or the next day. You'll have to hand over your guns or turn around."

The skinny man was out to Underwood's right. "That star-toter has got a one-track mind, Mr. Underwood. He kept on telling me that same foolishness a while ago."

"We are Christian men," the old man said, "and they ain't no call for bloodshed. We got you all outnumbered, Deputy. Get out of the way."

Youngblood couldn't tell whether the old man was bluffing or not; probably he hadn't made up his mind. It wouldn't hurt to try to influence him. "Mr. Underwood," he said, "Some of your men may go through here with their guns, but I'm sure you won't. If you don't think I can hit you from here, you don't know me very well. I've shot crows out of the air at twice this distance with this same gun. If you don't believe me, just try me. I mean to drill you plum dead center. Now make up your mind. Turn over your guns or turn around and go home."

Ogle spoke up from the rear. "Perhaps . . . uh . . . Mr. Underwood, we shouldn't press the matter at this time. Perhaps there are other ways . . ."

Underwood's puckered mouth was drawn into a thin straight line. He was a stubborn man. Perhaps he would have backed down if Ogle had not spoken. He jerked his head sideways slightly, and the skinny cowboy's horse began to jerk at the reins and prance nervously to the side. The movement might have appeared uncalculated to a casual observer, but the deputy knew better; the cowboy's left boot and spur were gripping too close to the flank and he was holding up too hard on a tender mouth. The movement was taking the skinny cowboy so far to the side that Youngblood could not clearly see him and Underwood both.

The deputy dipped his gun quickly and triggered off a shot into the dirt in front of and outside of the skittering horse, sending a shower of dust into his path. He prayed as he did it that the men behind him would remember their orders and hold their fire.

"Bring that horse back in here, cowboy," he said. He had turned his aim back to the old man, the hammer of his .44 quickly cocked again. "Underwood, you are fixing to get somebody killed."

Ogle was starting to say something when the skinny cowboy made his play. Youngblood saw only the flick of his wrist and his gun rising above the saddle. They fired together.

The deputy felt a tug at his hat and a tug at his scalp just over his right ear, but his own shot had found its mark. The cowboy went sprawling back over his horse's rump. Old Eb's shotgun boomed, but in the melee of rearing horses no one fell. The drygoods clerk fired twice. Ogle's horse fell dead and he scrambled on foot back toward the retreating riders.

The skinny cowboy rolled back and forth on the ground gripping his left shoulder with his right hand. He screamed, "Help me! I'm dying!" His nervous horse ran back with the others.

Underwood had his gun in his hand, but the deputy could see his uncertainty. The old man called, "Let me get my wounded man!"

"Throw down your guns!" Youngblood commanded.

Ogle was running among the horsemen trying to catch the loose horse. Underwood holstered his gun; the other two followed suit.

"I said throw them down!" the deputy repeated. "Into the dirt!"

"For God's sake, help me, Mr. Underwood," the skinny cowboy begged.

Underwood started forward. "We done changed our mind, Deputy. Let us get our wounded. We ain't going to town."

"You'll not go anywhere if you don't drop your guns," Youngblood insisted.

Underwood screamed, "Ain't you got no Christian mercy? A man dying on the ground and you still asking for a fight?" He threw his gun angrily to the ground.

The deputy had felt the tug at his hair and then a burning in his scalp behind his ear. Now he was surprised to feel the tickling of blood going down the back of his collar. He knew the wounded cowboy was not dying, because he was rolling around too much. "Hold it, Underwood," he said. "Go back to your horse and get that carbine out of that scabbard and throw it down, too, and tell your other men to throw down their guns."

They finally all complied, except Ogle, who was still occupied with the loose horse, then came forward and

124

picked up the skinny cowboy and loaded him into a saddle. He was pale and shaky; his shoulder was covered with blood caked with dirt. Ogle's hand mounted behind the wounded man to hold him in the saddle.

Old man Underwood said, "You sure ain't heard the last of this, young man! We only fired once, and you all fired at least four times. Before the sun goes down tomorrow, you're going to wish you could get out of the fight with just a shoulder wound."

"I'm proud we fired four times to your once," Youngblood told him. "Maybe you ought to think about that a little bit. Now, get out of here before I place you under arrest." He was waiting anxiously for them to turn their backs so he could feel of his head.

Underwood led them back the way they had come. The wounded cowboy begged to be taken to town to the doc, almost cried, but his stern old boss seemed to pay no heed.

Youngblood fingered his head and found that he had a gash two inches long in his scalp. The drygoods clerk tore the tail off his white shirt, and they bound up the deputy's head to stop the bleeding. Smitty thought the three of them could handle their position if the deputy wanted to go back to town, but Youngblood shook his head. "You know, I think I've made a mistake," he said. "I should have arrested that old man and taken him to town. I wish we had talked that over with the sheriff. I bet we could jail a half dozen ranchers and cool this whole trouble down, and Underwood is one of the half dozen."

He had been watching the riders as they went back the way they came. Now they were veering off the road toward the west. "I wish you fellers would pick up those guns they left us and then stick around. I'm going to do a little more looking."

He got his horse again and rode down the creek bed to a cattle crossing, where he turned out west, and rode back to the high ground he had been on an hour before. He had thought Underwood's group might for some reason be making a big circle to go into town, but they were riding toward the fence corner he had noted before, still walking their horses. They turned west up the fence. Somewhere within three miles of the corner must be a gate. Underwood was taking his bunch to the Rail-P.

Youngblood settled the clumsy bandage more firmly

around his head and rode down to the creek again. They turned back one more lone rider before they were relieved by Slim and three others in the middle of the afternoon.

Back in town the deputy found that the stations on the other roads into town had been successful. Some twenty ranchers had been turned back. Only two cowboys had surrendered their guns willingly. They had hung around, had a couple of drinks at McSween's, then rode on west toward the spread of Stephen Pendergrass, the Rail-P.

Chapter 15

THE JUDGE had pulled his chair over to the window of his office and was sitting watching main street. His door was open to take advantage of any breeze that might come along the hall. He looked up and saw the tall heavy figure of his brother in the doorway and wondered how long he had been there; it wasn't like Stephen to stand waiting silently.

The judge had conflicting impulses. It would have been natural for him to ask, What can I do for you? He had a stronger impulse to tell Steve to go away, beg him to go away and not press their differences further. Already, it seemed, they had argued so violently that they could never be at ease with each other again. But he had tried to stop the arguments before and had failed. There was something about it all that he did not understand. His brother would argue until they came to an impasse, then become violently angry, but return to argue again like a man obsessed. It was not only that the judge did not understand; he had a *need* to understand because of the bribe attempt; it somehow required a lot of understanding, even though he was certain that it could never be justified.

When Steve spoke he seemed straining to be casual. "I see your big detachment of precious Rangers has arrived."

"Yes, they have arrived."

126

"They look like a pitiful bunch to do what you expect them to do."

"They look like fine men to me," the judge said.

"Four men!" Steve said sarcastically, but still not saying what he had come to say.

"Perhaps Lieutenant Ruth has telegraphed for reinforcements."

"If he has they won't get here in time."

"Perhaps not. Unless they happened to be in Colorado City." The judge threw out this misleading hint, not even caring greatly whether he fooled his brother or not. He felt strongly his need to understand the big man and his obsession and even imagined that he could see in the proud face of his brother some sign of weakness. The man stood in the doorway a half minute saying nothing.

"Come in, Steve," the judge said. "Take a seat. I've been thinking about asking you a couple of questions in regard to our conversation down at the bank the other day."

The big man came in and sat down. "I don't remember our conversation and don't care to," he announced.

The judge pressed the matter. "You said something about the pride you took in the Battle of San Jacinto. I talked to someone who works for you and you know what he told me? He said, "Sure, everybody knows Mr. Pendergrass fought at the Battle of San Jacinto.'"

"Well, so what?" the big man said. "Why do you bring up an argument that's finished?"

"I just wondered if you fought at the Alamo too."

"What are you trying to do?" the big man said, his face flushed. "What do you know about it? You were just a kid."

"A kid? Where are you, Steve? In some kind of dream world? I was twelve and you were thirteen. You were not fourteen till the following December. Don't you think I remember when Pa came home from the big battle and gave you a whipping because you didn't have the corn in? He had laid out our tasks for us, and you hadn't planted the corn, which was your job, and Ma made an excuse for you, but Pa whipped you anyway. You ran away from home and stayed away three weeks. Don't you think I remember that? You ask me what I'm trying to do. What are *you* trying to do? Have you built up a fine repu-

127

tation based on lies and then come to believe them yourself?"

The big man repeated, "What are you trying to do? I don't see what all this has got to do with our disagreement, and I don't see why you think it's your business."

"Do you believe that you fought at San Jacinto?"

The big man did not answer.

"I'll tell you what I'm trying to do, Steve. I'm trying to understand you. I've seen you go in one short month from a man I respected to a man in whom I see very little to respect. If you are living in a foolish dream, it's time to wake up. Maybe this San Jacinto business is just a minor lie that you didn't start—maybe you have just allowed people to jump to conclusions. On the other hand, maybe you have built yourself up into a big fraud and have become blind to facts."

The big man had changed so that there was no casual air about him, strained or otherwise, and no hint of weakness. He was angry but for once was suppressing it. "I'm afraid you're going to be surprised when you find out who's dreaming and who's facing facts."

"I'm honestly trying to understand you, Steve."

"I came here to tell you something and you don't make it easy with all this slander."

"If it's about yourself, tell me," the judge said. "But if it's some more bull about how good Ivey is, never mind."

"I'll have to ask you to keep it secret. Give me your word."

The judge studied him. "I think not, Steve. If you're going to tell me, tell me. I doubt that it's of importance to me anyway; you and I don't agree about what's important."

"You'll agree it's important when I tell you, and you'll see why I couldn't tell you unless you give your word to keep it secret."

"Is it about Ivey?"

"It's about the possibility of me withdrawing from this fight. Today is July 30th, Albert. Do you know what that means?"

"Yes, I know what it means. Ivey hasn't got much time."

"What it means is this: today is the last day this thing can be settled without a lot of bloodshed."

"If that's still your attitude, perhaps we'd better let the matter drop," the judge told him. "You're still asking the law to compromise."

"No, I'm not. All I'm asking is for my own brother to keep a secret I tell him, and if you won't, I want you to remember I tried my best to convince you. I think you'll be sorry some day you wouldn't do even this for me."

"What if I learn it some other way, after you have told me?"

"I'll gamble on it," the big man said. "If you find out some place else, you can do whatever you please."

"All right, I'll give you my word. I'll keep it secret unless I find out from another source."

The big man settled back. He was still angry but seemed relieved, as if he had finally gotten around to the purpose of his visit. "I'm the man that paid Ivey to kill Dudley and Brown and the rest. Just five. I think you know that Ivey has been charged with killings he couldn't possibly have done. I had plenty of reason for making the deal with him, whether you agree or not; at least we cut out the rustling."

"You paid him to shoot them in the back?"

"That's right. I don't figure the men he killed had a square deal coming. I fixed up his alibis and I paid him six hundred dollars a head."

"Why do you tell me such things as this, Steve?"

"Because if you can think about Ivey just one time without getting so self-righteous you'll see him in a new light. You don't blame him for killing Indians. You don't blame him for killing lawbreakers in the line of duty when he was a deputy marshal. Now these fellers were rustlers and he was paid to do a job by the most respected man in this part of the country. You talk about bucking authority. Albert, *I* was the authority in the eyes of William Ivey and still am for more people around here than you realize. You talk about history. I tell you there's been vigilante action on the American frontier for two hundred years. Why do you pick out Ivey's action to damn? He's done some legal killing and others so near legal that people who hate rustling can't tell the difference.

"That's why I say I know he didn't kill the damn sheepherder's kid. I know who he killed. I fixed up his alibis and I paid him."

The judge had been carefully studying his brother's face. "Steve," he said slowly, "I want you to know that I don't believe you and I'm happy that I don't, real happy."

"Don't believe me! What do you mean? How could I possibly expect to benefit..."

"You expect to make Ivey look like an admirable person. You are still trying every way to save him. But I'm not interested in Ivey. I'm trying to understand *you*. I think I know one thing about you—you have a code; you don't shoot people in the back. I don't think my opinion here depends on our being brothers either. I just don't think you pay to have people shot in the back. What I don't understand is why you will go to such lengths to free Ivey. Why do you return and return to me, even swallow your pride, to pursue our argument?"

"I've told you why, and if Ivey mounts that scaffold day after tomorrow, he's going to tell the world."

"Steve, surely to God you are not guilty of what you claim. Listen, I have a revelation to make, and I don't want you to keep it secret. I want you to tell the other ranchers what they are fighting about. I hope you tell the man who paid Ivey, if you know who he is, so he'll know for sure what his despicable vigilante deal has finally led on. Ivey has confessed to killing the Munson boy and he was telling the truth. Almost casually he killed the child. He was no more sorry for having done it than you would be for having killed a coyote."

Now the big man revealed his anger in his voice. "That's a lie! I know Ivey better than that; it was a business with him. He killed for money maybe, but he didn't kill for fun."

"No, he killed the boy by mistake, but he made the mistake because he was trying to kill the boy's father for a simple insult. The man who hired Ivey to shoot men in the back turned loose a monster in the country."

"You're lying! You're still trying to get me to back down with fancy words." The big man rose. He was talking loudly now and shaking in his anger. "If you've got half the sense you're supposed to have, you'll be able to see I can't allow Ivey to mount that scaffold." He brought his fist down on the desk of the judge with a bang, so that the floor itself shook. "You know who the leader of the ranchers is around here. You're looking at him. And if you think I'm going to back down then you don't know how I got where I am today." There was something final in the action of Steve Pendergrass as he walked out, and a resolution; he had made up his mind on some course of action.

Before his brother had come in, the judge had been dividing his attention between a journal he was reading and the main street of town. Now he paid attention to neither. He was searching in his mind for some indication of truth or falsity in Steve's confession. If his brother were guilty of paying Ivey, it would explain his obsession. But perhaps just plain stubbornness would, too. And there was the code. Wasn't it true that people such as Steve made it a point of honor not to shoot a man in the back? Or was that a myth? Or was it a point of honor that extended only to cattlemen and not to inferior ordinary people? Certainly *some* rancher had failed to follow any such code and had paid Ivey, knowing that he was shooting men in the back. He had to accept that *some* rancher had done it, so he could not logically deny that Steve had done it, on the basis that ranchers don't do such things. His belief that Steve was incapable of it must come from the fact that Steve was his brother, and the judge knew that such beliefs have a peculiar weakness. How many times he had seen a mother swear that her son could not possibly have committed a crime which her son most certainly had committed. But these thoughts did not prove anything. There was always the possibility that Steve was maneuvering as a front for someone else. He clung to that hope.

Deputy Youngblood had slept until midnight and now he was on duty alone at the sheriff's office. The town was quiet. He paced the office, stood in the doorway, and occasionally walked out into the street. Here and there at the front of the buildings hung a kerosene lantern, turned low, and farther down were the fancy lights of the White Plaza and the Robert Lee Hotel. But the broad street was empty from hitch rail to hitch rail as for down as he could see.

He was thinking about writing a letter. The idea had come to him because of the quiet and loneliness and because of the rip in his scalp, which had become sore to

131

the touch through the bandage the doc had put on. If the bullet had been just an inch farther over ... He had intended to go out to the house to see Lila when he was finished with his duties the evening before, but the sheriff had said to them, "I want all of you to hit that bunk and get as much sleep as you can. If I don't miss my guess, we'll be plenty shorthanded for the job we've got ahead of us tomorrow." And since there had been no real necessity that he go to Lila, he had not pressed the matter.

He didn't know exactly what he wanted to say in a letter. He could say that here on this last day of July in this quiet moment she was in his thoughts, and if anything happened to him she was to stay with Uncle Charlie and Aunt Annie. He had a more uncertain idea, too, of writing to a child that he might never see. The letter could be given him or her, in fifteen or eighteen years. That would be past the turn of the century. Nineteen hundred! What a different life the child would lead!

He went so far as to lay a sheet of blank paper down on the sheriff's desk and dip a pen into ink, but the letters never got written. To write them would be to admit something he wasn't ready to admit. He had no intentions of stopping any lead. Whatever he could write to Lila, she knew already, and whatever he could write to a child would be told the child better than he could tell it, by someone who knew the outcome and final meaning of the events he was a part of. There was only one thing he really wanted to say to the child: that he was serious about what he was doing. He carried a knife scar in his thigh from a roughhouse in Dodge; the man had actually meant to kill him, and it had been nothing but youthful foolishness. But today, this wasn't like that. He knew what he was doing, had had a chance to get out, knew the risk, believed it was worth doing. How could you put such things into words? Any words you used would look plenty silly at daybreak.

A little after two o'clock in the morning Slim came in from the post on the south road. He held his horse in front of the door and talked to Youngblood.

"How did it go out there?" Youngblood asked.

"Plum quiet since dark," the slender deputy said. "We

132

turned back two fellers after you left, and one got past us, that Mexican Torres."

"Was he armed?"

"I don't know. I didn't get that close to him. He didn't come by the road. But I reckon he was. I never saw him but what he had a gun on."

"Me neither, but I wouldn't worry about it."

"He gives me the creeps," Slim said. "You never know where he's going to turn up, but you derned sure ain't going to get close to him. Reckon the sheriff would want me to try to look him up and take his gun? He's probably out there in the Mex quarter somewheres."

"I don't think so. You couldn't do any good this time of night without waking up a lot of people. Why don't you feed your horse and get some sleep. I get the idea the sheriff may roust you out about daylight."

Chapter 16

STEPHEN PENDERGRASS looked like a banker when he rode out of town that morning in a custom-built hack, past his fine, white town house and out into the grassland of the Rail-P. He was a banker, almost a dude, stiff and formal in his black suit, white shirt, black string tie, and derby. He had a cruious desperate look in his dignity, perhaps like a banker who has lost his bank.

Later that afternoon he had changed his appearance. He spoke to the assembled riders briefly, raised his right hand and thrust it toward where Comanche Wells lay, five miles across the plains, and led them out. Now he looked as he had in years past, almost a part of the giant black horse he rode, dressed in range clothes, on his head a broad-brimmed black stetson.

He seemed to belong at their front because of a grandeur that clung to his person, but his command of them was not so much like that of a strict military officer as like that of an avenging cossack leader.

His horse moved in a fast trot, causing some of the

smaller horses behind him to break into a lope at times to keep the pace.

They were thirty-seven riders, armed with sideguns, and most with rifles, stuck in a saddle boot or carried across the cantle. They rode bunched and strung out to each side to avoid eating the dust they raised. They seemed all of one purpose, a selected group.

Some men, like Long, were absent because they were neutral. Some men, like Moss, were absent because they were plainly against it. Some men, like Ogle, were absent because they were not wanted. Some good cowhands, who also happened to be good with a gun, had been fired because they were unwilling to ride with the bunch. These thirty-seven rode with various fires behind their common purpose: Bledsoe believed that they were deciding the future of the West; Underwood believed that God was on his side. All of them felt sure they were right. And each of them had in his attitude the words, "Now, at last, we are through playing around." This attitude was related to their feeling about the powerful old man who towered in front of them, Stephen Pendergrass.

If the banker had changed that day, so had the town. The sheriff had spread his men thinly with only one at the jail and only one at each of the other approaches to town—except for the west road; here, on the road that led nowhere except to the vast Rail-P, he had sixteen lawmen and posse members. The townsmen on the posse had changed, not much in ability but in confidence. The day before they had held guns on cattlemen and seen them turn back. It would be rougher today, but their faith in the calm lawmen they worked with had grown.

The sheriff had agreed to Youngblood's idea that certain of the ranchers, such as Underwood, should be arrested instead of driven back, if the opportunity came. He had arranged for a strong storm cellar to keep any such prisoners in. He also agreed with the advice the judge had given: "At long range, go for their horses. A cowboy will ride into hell on horseback, but he won't walk into much of anything."

Youngblood squatted on the ground among the others, staring at the broad expanse of prairie divided by the road. It was a cruelly open place for a gunfight. Behind them was a thicket of mesquite and chaparral in which they had left their horses. For cover they had the remains where a house had been, with some few rotten timbers, and across the road, the remains of some smaller structure, with a few broken tree limbs. But ahead of them was no cover at all bigger than a bunch of grass.

A mile out he could see the tall proud gate of the Rail-P's main entrance. It was past noon when the riders came pouring through. The sheriff stood up and said, "On your feet, everybody! Don't take cover till they get a good look at us. I aim for them to know what they face."

Then when the attackers were still nearly a half mile away, they charged, waving their guns and firing wildly. Their yells came faintly to the men on the road; their shots sounded like toy guns popping.

"The fools!" the sheriff said. "They must think we'll run! I sure never thought they'd make it this easy. Take what cover you can find, and hold your fire till they get in range."

Youngblood dashed to the other side of the road and flopped to his belly behind a wooden chunk ten inches thick. He was followed by four others. He lined his rifle sights on the thundering riders. A slug fell with a plunk in the road. The deputy sighted on a dark horse that stood out against the red dust the charging riders raised. There was little wind; he allowed about two feet bullet drop and squeezed the trigger. The black horse came on. Rifles began to crack from other positions beside the road.

The oncoming riders grew large in their field of vision. The deputy sighted on a big paint that was coming straight and squeezed the trigger again. The paint somersaulted and flung his rider, spread-eagle, ahead of him.

"God! did you see that man leave that saddle?" someone behind him said.

"I bet he lost some skin when he hit the ground," another said.

A slug tore into Youngblood's protective chunk, slamming it aside. He rolled over behind it. Everyone was blasting away now. Powder smoke clung around them in the hot air.

Among the ranchers another rider was picked from the saddle as if by an invisible noose and lay still on the ground. A horse slid to a halt on his back feet, then sank to his knees. A tall rider who had been waving his hot six-gun wildly in the air suddenly clawed leather, but the strength had gone out of him and he fell. He was picked up by another rider. Then a hundred yards from them the attacking wave broke and turned. They still fired as they went back. Their bullets raised their spits of dust among the lawmen and possemen.

Youngblood had seen that the leader was Stephen Pendergrass. He tried to find him in his rifle sights, but their retreat was covered by their own dust. He raised up on his elbow and looked at the four men around him; none of them was hurt. Right behind him the drygoods clerk grinned broadly.

As the dust settled out ahead he saw that the ranchers had stopped and were unlimbering their rifles, beginning to fire across saddle seats. He heard the sheriff yell, "Keep your damn heads down!"

The fire from the ranchers proved ineffective at the range, and the deputy began to look for them to try something else. Then he could tell that an argument had sprung up among them. Their angry voices came faintly across the distance. One cattleman mounted and came toward the roadblock at a lope, with a white handkerchief fluttering from upheld rifle.

"Hold your fire!" the sheriff yelled, "but keep down!"

The rider was Bledsoe. He drew up at the body of the dead rancher and looked down at it a moment without dismounting, then came on. The sheriff let him ride right up among them before he rose and faced him with drawn .44. He said, "Climb down out of that saddle, Bledsoe."

"I come up here under a flag of truce," the heavy rancher said. "You see we mean business. I'm going against some them men out there, even Pendergrass. They aim to wipe you out, but I figure you got enough sense to see you're beaten."

"I don't give a hoot for your white rag," the sheriff said. "Get down or I'll shoot you down!"

"I came up here under a flag of truce!"

"You're resisting arrest, Bledsoe. This ain't no game we're playing. What the hell makes you think you got right to declare war on the law in the first place? Now, get down or, so help me, I'll kill you!"

The heavy man dismounted and the sheriff snapped on

handcuffs. The rancher sputtered, aghast at the lack of respect for the flag of truce. The sheriff said, "Andy, take him to town and throw him in that cellar. Here's the key. Get back as soon as you can."

The ranchers began firing again and were answered by the sheriff's men. Another horse was hit; the animal's high scream died away as it kicked feebly on the ground. The cattlemen mounted and pulled back, but left at least two men with rifles behind the now motionless body of the horse. The riders were turning south.

The sheriff came running across the road and grunted as he fell on his belly beside Youngblood. "I'm going to leave one posseman here with a rifle. The rest of us will make a run for the horses. Now, we may get split up; what we got to do is stay between that bunch and town." He added as an afterthought, in a voice that was like a growl, "I was to get winged or something, you're in charge, but listen to Judge Pendergrass and Lieutenant Ruth."

They dashed back toward the thicket and the horses two or three at a time. Here and there a bullet clipped through the skinny limbs. They mounted and rode out in a long string toward the brakes of Seedy Creek to the south. Youngblood started off about the middle but spurred up toward the front where the sheriff was. His superior was choosing their route carefully. The cattlemen were riding around a larger circle, but the sheriff's men, being outnumbered, had to be able to take cover. And they had to avoid being penned down.

Both of the bunches became scattered in the rough country near the creek. Youngblood found himself at the lead of four possemen. He came almost to the top of a rise and suddenly faced a massed group of eight or ten ranchers. He blasted away at them and led his men in a hard race for the creek bed amidst a hail of bullets. One of the ranchers tumbled from his horse and another slumped down, clutching the saddle horn. They went into the creek farther south.

In the creek Youngblood looked over his men. One of them, a Mexican who worked for the stage line, had blood streaming down his shirt sleeve. The deputy tore off the sleeve. It was a bad wound, clear through the bone of his upper arm. The deputy slowed the blood with a tight bandage made of the bloody sleeve. "Can you ride?" he asked.

The Mexican looked quite serious. His olive skin was pale. "Certainly, Senor Deputy."

"Are you weak? I'll send a man into town with you if you need him."

"No, Senor Deputy. I stay and fight some more."

"Like hell you will." They loaded him onto his horse. "Go straight to the doc, you hear," Youngblood said. The man rode down the gravelly creek bottom toward Comanche Wells, his wounded arm hanging as limp as if no bone were inside it.

The bunch of ranchers came probing down the creek, and Youngblood and his remaining three turned them back with a fierce fusilade. It was quiet for a minute. They could hear scattered shots to the south, then a burst of firing to the southeast, maybe a half mile away. The deputy climbed cautiously up the bank and looked around. To the south and west he saw a rider going away, leading a horse with a form face down across a saddle. Out to the east he could see the main group of the sheriff's men and farther away from town drifting dust that marked more riders. Youngblood climbed back down the bank and led his men in a search for a quarter of a mile along the creek and, finding nothing, cut out east to join the sheriff.

After the sheriff heard about the two cattlemen Youngblood knew were out of action, he said, "I don't believe we lost track of any of them around the creek. This bunch you see out there must be the ones you run into. There's about twenty more circling farther out with Pendergrass."

They rode on east and then slanted north. The sheriff was concerned because they could not see the largest group of attackers, however they did have a fair view of all the approaches to town. "At least they ain't got quite the odds they had," he told Youngblood. "Two of them fellers in that bunch are carrying lead."

They rode for half an hour till they were due east of Comanche Wells, then they saw a rider coming hell-for-leather out of town to intercept them. The man was coming as fast as Youngblood had ever seen a horse move. He rode curiously like a race jockey, only with a sideways twist to his body as if he had lost one stirrup. There was something familiar about the small figure. It was Judge Pendergrass. His cotton suit was a wrinkled mess; his hair, a grizzled mat on his barehead.

"Bunch of riders north of town," he told the sheriff breathlessly. "About twenty." He took off his brass-rimmed spectacles with one hand and wiped some of the dust from them against his coat.

"My God!" the sheriff said. "They've really been riding! One good thing, our horses ain't worn out like theirs must be. How far would you say?"

"Nearly two miles from the courthouse."

The sheriff turned to Lieutenant Ruth. "I make seven men out yonder, at least two of them bad wounded. And they ain't anything but a decoy. Can you hold them back with two men, three counting you?"

"I believe so."

"Take one of your men and Jones back there. The rest of you, let's go." He led them in an easy lope toward town. He had picked up three men at guard points in his circle of town and now had fourteen men to face the twenty. The odds were still improving.

The judge rode between the sheriff and Youngblood. He said, grunting with the gait of his horse, "I'd like you to swear me in, Sheriff."

"Swear you in?"

"As a posse member."

The sheriff grinned but saw that the judge wasn't joking.

"At least," the judge went on, "let me take Slim's place at the jail. I'll send him to help you."

"Raise your right hand."

At this the judge grinned. "You want me to fall off this horse? Let's say I've got it raised spiritually if not physically."

The sheriff repeated the oath, phrase by phrase, and the judge echoed it, the same words the sheriff had used with fourteen of the townsmen during the previous week. To Youngblood, there was irony in it that should be funny but wasn't; the judge had taught the oath to the sheriff in the first place.

They came into the north edge of town and turned up into the high ground. When they topped the second rise, only a quarter of a mile above the courthouse, they could see the bunch coming witth Stephen Pendergrass at their head. It was here that the fight was fiercely pressed home, for the ranchers, met with strength after their long circle, seemed at last to accept that they faced a worthy foe

139

and might be beaten unless they were willing to pay for victory.

Over and over Stephen Pendergrass led his men in a charge on their lathered, dust-caked horses, tried to turn the sheriff's flank, saw his men fall from the saddles, and retreated, moved west, and tried again. Once over a ridge Youngblood could hear loud cursing from the big ranch leader, and a few minutes later he saw three cowboys riding away, sick of the battle. As they moved west, the deputy passed across a shallow arroya where the latest charge had faltered and saw Underwood's body, face up to the sky, a bullet hole in his forehead. The gaunt old man's lips were puckered as if he might yet voice some shrill acid-like demand.

In a lull two ranch men came on foot carrying a badly bleeding friend, wanting to get him to the doctor. One of the bearers was Burge, ex-sheriff Long's top hand. The sheriff took their guns and put them in the charge of a posseman, who was to see that they went into the storm cellar when their errand of mercy was finished.

They were northwest of town, where the land began to slope off level, when Stephen Pendergrass made his last attempt to get through. He had made almost a complete circle of the town. His horses were nervous in their weakness; they kept falling to their knees on the slopes.

Deputy Youngblood had dismounted at the top of the rise with old Eb, the blacksmith. They had some cover from two live oak trees. He cautioned the old man to come back and take cover as the riders came within range. He fired three times and saw a rider drop, then ran out after the blacksmith, but he was too late. The old man fell and was clumsily trying to load his shotgun when he was hit again with a slug that seemed to slam him into the dirt. Youngblood dragged him back, but it was useless. Old Eb died nodding his head, clutching his gun, and trying to say something. The deputy thought he was trying to say that they were winning.

The sheriff came along the rise and said to Youngblood, "Pendergrass is pulling away to the west. I think he's done, but I aim to watch him a while. We left a wounded Ranger back yonder a ways; you want to go back and make sure he gets to the doc?"

"What about Ruth?" the deputy asked, "and the cattlemen he was watching?"

"Ruth is right down there in the ravine," the sheriff

140

told him. "Those cattlemen joined Pendergrass before that last damned rush. That's all of them, boy. That's all there is."

Pendergrass rode west. Of his original number, four of the most aggressive were locked in a dark storm cellar in town; three lay dead and untended along the route of their fighting; nine were wounded seriously; some had gone back to help the wounded get to a ranch where they would be cared for; less than a half-dozen had deserted their leader. But of the thirty-seven who had followed him toward town, only seven rode with him back west.

Youngblood stood on the high ground northwest of town as dusk came. The drygoods clerk was with him. They served as lookouts. The deputy felt the strangeness of the quiet and the lack of movement. His ears still rang from the gunfire, and sounds such as his horse cropping grass came to him muffled. The drygoods clerk did not chatter as he had the day before just to hear the sound of his voice.

After some time of silence the clerk said, "Mr. Youngblood." To the deputy the "Mister" sounded strange; the clerk was about as old as he was. "Mr. Youngblood, you know, I really thought that Ivey should be hanged, but I didn't believe you all could actually do it. Now, I believe you all actually will."

Youngblood said quietly, "I reckon we will."

Chapter 17

AUGUST THE FIRST dawned clear without even the trace of a wispy cloud overhead. The air was still, and by mid-morning one of the hottest days of a hot, dry climate was in progress. The sky was pale blue-gray, deceptively pale, for if one were to stare into it, even with his back to the sun, perhaps to follow the flight of a hawk, he would have found himself squinting and his eyes watering from the brightness.

141

The people of the town had begun to move toward the courthouse by mid-morning, toward the open area at the north end of the building where the rough wooden scaffold had risen, with its heavy rope already suspended from the top crossbeam, the noose already formed, the big crude knot black against the hot sky. They were thinking that by coming early they would find a favorable spot from which to observe the proceedings, not too far away yet not too close. The town was turning out in force. The month-long struggle to hold Ivey had kindled the interest of even the least civic minded, and the engagement of so many townspeople in the sheriff's special stand-by posse had fanned the flame of interest to a high pitch. Most of those who would not go had been forbidden. Some wives were forbidden with the words: "It ain't no place for a woman." Many children were forbidden with the words: "No, you certainly may not; it's not a sight for children's eyes." But curiously some equally righteous parents brought their children, determined that they should observe the wages of sin.

Some children, perhaps forbidden to go, observed from a distance. As the hour wore on toward noon, figures appeared on the rooftops of well-situated houses, and out on McWilliams' windmill and metal water tank a group of boys perched. Some older boys had taken a position on the roof of the hardware store across the street from the courthouse. The plank fence of the sheriff's corral furnished a seat for people of all ages.

As they milled about in the open area, staying back from the scaffold itself, some people chatted gaily with their neighbors, as if they were about to see a circus; others stayed silent and looked serious. Similarly, their dress contrasted: some wore casual everyday clothes, or even dirty work clothes; others wore their best, as if for church.

The gay women of the town turned out in their frizzled hair and finery, those who worked at the White Plaza and at McSween's and those who worked only in their shacks out east of town. It was the first time in months for most of them to be out of bed before noon.

Mexican men came without any of their women, though some brought their male children. They gathered in a

142

knot apart from the others and conversed in their quick passionate Spanish.

The bright sun was the master of all the people. They talked of the heat and sweated and waited. Many copies of the *Courier* were in evidence, as fans, as shades for the eyes, as covers over the head. A group of five dogs of all sizes and colors had come to be a part of the crowd. They ran about smelling of each other, gaily chasing and snarling and following. One of them, a spotted hound with mournful face took refuge from the sun in the shade under the platform of the scaffold. He lay a moment, then rose and, squatting with his nose pointed up, howled long and mournfully. There was general laughter from the crowd, but here and there a person frowned and shook his head superstitiously. The Mexicans stopped their chatter, stared at the hound, and stared at each other, then cut their eyes around uneasily.

The sheriff had disposed his forces according to two thoughts: first that their prisoner might still be rescued and second that it was the responsibility of the sheriff's department and not the Rangers to perform the duty assigned by the district court sitting in Comanche Wells a month ago. Accordingly he sent Lieutenant Ruth and two Rangers to lead three small mounted posses, patrolling the outskirts of town and watching the roads. They were to go no more than a half-mile from town so they could hear gunfire and return if needed. The sheriff kept his own deputies at hand to guard the person of the prisoner and carry out the court order.

Not long after breakfast the Baptist preacher had gone alone up to Ivey's cell. He had wanted to carry the key so that he might enter the cell and have a closer contact with the condemned man, but the sheriff had vetoed such an idea with words that could not be misunderstood. The preacher did not stay long upstairs. He came down greatly flustered with the starched front of his white shirt torn out, feeling lucky that he had not been choked to death and vowing that Ivey could go to hell. He would remain ready to offer spiritual comfort if it were asked for but would not come within reach of the man again.

At eleven o'clock the sheriff was ready to begin, but

143

Judge Pendergrass came down the corridor to the office with news to delay them. He said, "Sheriff, my brother is in town. I have seen him standing in the door of the bank."

"By his self?"

"I saw only him."

The sheriff scratched his head. "Well, do you think it means anything? He's not liable to try to break Ivey loose by his self, is he?"

"I don't know," the judge said, then added, speaking slowly and deliberately, "I must tell you, Sheriff, what I should have told you before. My brother confessed to me two days ago that he is the man who paid Ivey. I honestly thought it was a lie, but since yesterday I am not sure."

The lawmen were surprised. Youngblood could see from the lines in the judge's face that the knowledge and the telling of it were costing the old man. He had not thought of the judge as an old man before, because of the youthfulness of his ideas and the animation of his face.

"I don't know what he might do," the judge went on, "but I think you must reckon with the possibility that he might make a desperate attempt to break Ivey loose, or he might shoot him to prevent his talking."

"Youngblood," the sheriff said. "Get over to the bank right away. I want to know who all is in there. If you have to break a window or something, go ahead. I'll take the blame."

"Do you want Mr. Pendergrass arrested?"

"We don't have time now. Just check. Get going."

The deputy hurried up the street. The town seemed empty. He walked in the dirt of the street instead of on the board walks in order to make as little noise as possible. When he came in front of the bank, he saw what seemed to be a slight movement of the door as if it had been open a crack and were being closed. Youngblood sprang upon the porch and set his shoulder against the door as he wrenched at the knob. The door yielded. As he went in, he saw Mr. Stephen Pendergrass stagger back, pushed by the door. The big man's face was white as if he were sick; he seemed at a complete loss.

"Are you alone?" the deputy demanded.

144

"Get out of here!"

Youngblood repeated, "Are you alone?"

The banker was not armed. The deputy ran around him and peered quickly behind the barred cage and into the offices in the rear. The man was alone. Youngblood left as quickly as he had come in. He had spent no more than fifteen seconds in the bank.

Back at the courthouse, the sheriff heard his report and asked, "Did he have a gun on him?"

"No sir, but of course he probably has one in the bank. I didn't search the place that close."

"All right. Let's go get Ivey." The sheriff took a pair of handcuffs from his desk and wadded a length of small rope into his back pocket.

The judge went ahead outside and the four lawmen trooped up the stairs. In front of the cell, the sheriff stopped to fish the key out of his pockets and said, "Get up, Ivey. The time has come."

"Time for what? I want to see Steve Pendergrass."

"I'm afraid it's too late for anything like that, feller. Get up!"

"Hold on, Sheriff, God dammit! I'll make a deal with you. Where is Pendergrass?"

"What do you care where he is? And you won't make no deal with me neither, Ivey. I don't guess it's sunk through that thick head of yours, but you got a debt to pay, and the time has come, and there ain't no way around it at all."

They seized him by the arms, brought them together behind him, and snapped on the cuffs.

"Hold on, God dammit! Listen to my deal! I'll name the man that paid me to kill Brown and Dudley and the rest."

"You name him when you get ready, but it'll do more good if you wait till you're in front of that crowd outside."

"Will you put off this damn hanging and give me some kind of a chance? At least give me some kind of a run for it?"

The sheriff's voice was less harsh than it had been at any time in speaking to the prisoner during the past month "No, Ivey, I won't. Your time has come, and there ain't no way around it at all."

"Wait! Listen! Ain't I got no right? Where's that

145

damned dude lawyer that's supposed to look out for my rights?"

"He run out on you," the sheriff said. "You know that. Listen, feller, you can go the easy way, or you can go the hard way, but you got to go, one way or the other. Slim, you take a-holt of that arm, and Andy, you get this one, and don't you all let go for any reason till he's standing on that trap. Youngblood, I want you to go on outside. Take one rifle and make sure it's loaded. I want you to make sure we got a clear path, and then I want you to get on that platform and keep your eyes open; watch out for anything that might cause trouble."

As he went down the stairs, Youngblood could hear them scuffling with the prisoner as they brought him out of the cell. Outside he found a wide path open, and around the gallows itself, a clearing in the crowd. Some people on the outside were pushing in, but those nearest in pushed back, shrinking away from the crude timber structure. When he appeared, carrying the rifle, the crowd quieted; first a wave of whispers passed back through them, then the silence, then sporadic talk as they saw that the prisoner was not in sight. Youngblood mounted the six feet of steps and walked around the platform looking. He saw nothing amiss.

The deputy knew many of the people assembled here, at least by sight. Judge Pendergrass was back near the courthouse talking to Doc and some of the county dignitaries, the county clerk, the county judge, a couple of the commissioners. Editor Pitts, wearing a green eye shade, was walking around with a pad of paper in his hand; he had removed his dirty apron for the occasion. Youngblood saw out at the edge of the crowd, alone, waiting, the sheepherder Munson. The man seemed not even a part of the crowd. He was leaning some of his weight against a scraggly mesquite tree, and his stance reminded Youngblood of the last time he had seen him out in that barren country with one foot on the grave of his wife and his long-handled shovel stuck into the red clay grave of his murdered son.

Charlie Moss came running from the street into the crowd, looking around, asking questions, obviously searching for someone. Youngblood shouted at him but his uncle did not hear. The deputy thought he had better not leave his post. Moss finally spied Doc and went directly to him. The deputy could not hear their conversation, but could see that there was some kind of argument. Moss began tugging at Doc's arm, but the doctor did not want to go and swung his hand toward the scaffold as if indicating that he would be needed here. Youngblood heard only three words, in his uncle's insistent voice: "No! Right now!" The county officials and Judge Pendergrass seemed to side against the doctor, waving him away. Then the doctor gave in and followed his uncle hurriedly.

Youngblood's first thought was that Doc was needed for one of the men who had been wounded in the fight the day before. Maybe one of them was losing blood, or . . . Then he thought about Lila and he felt helpless. He could remember her saying, "August the first. It's my time." And something about doctors never being right about the date. He tried to put it out of his mind, because he knew there was nothing he could do, even if he had been free to do something. Maybe it was just as well that he was busy. He told himself to stop his stupid, useless worrying about it, but the admonition had little effect. He paced around the platform, looking across as much of the town as he could see and out into the country to the north.

When Ivey was brought out, the hush spread across the crowd again as the word was whispered back. People craned their necks and stood on tiptoe to see him. Andy and Slim still had their holds on his arms and the sheriff came behind. The prisoner was arguing and digging his boot heels into the ground. The crowd gave him plenty of room but closed in behind them as they went. A man's voice came out of the crowd with the words, "He don't look so tough now, does he!"

The sheriff became exasperated with the delay. He grasped Ivey's legs and pushed the long-heeled boots roughly from his feet. The man wore no socks, and his feet were damp with sweat; they became covered with dirt as he was dragged forward. The crowd closed in behind the struggling men but took care not to step on the boots, avoiding them as if they were contaminated.

When they were by the steps, Youngblood asked the sheriff, "Don't you want me down there?" The sheriff grunted a "No," and they brought Ivey up without his dirty bare feet once touching the rough new plank steps. Andy and Slim were dripping with perspiration.

The sheriff came around to face his prisoner. "If you

147

got anything to say, say it right now, Ivey. But don't ask for any deals."

Ivey cursed him.

"If you want to ask for a preacher, or if you want to confess anything, get on with it. We ain't going to stand on much ceremony."

It was well that Youngblood had kept his vigil. Past the corner of the courthouse he could see two and a half blocks down the street to the bank. As soon as the figure came out the door, the deputy noticed him. It was the tall figure of Stephen Pendergrass, and the object in his hand was unmistakably a rifle or shotgun. Youngblood tapped the sheriff on the shoulder and pointed. The sheriff gazed, uncertain. "Maybe you better let me have the rifle," he said to the deputy. "It's my responsibility." They waited while the big man came slowly to the first cross street.

The clatter of hooves came sudden and loud. It was one rider, going fast. He came from that part of town hidden by the courthouse, perhaps from a block west of main street. When he hove into sight, riding straight toward Stephen Pendergrass, the watching lawmen recognized him at once. It was the Mexican Torres, his great-brimmed hat turned up in front from the wind of his horse's speed and a six-gun bearing level in his right hand.

The big banker stopped as if surprised and confused. He never raised the gun he carried.

The Mexican opened fire at fifty feet and got off six shots. It seemed as if he would run his falling quarry down, but in the last second he swerved his horse and leaning over, fired the sixth of the shots no more than two feet from his target.

At this, Ivey, still held fast, gritted, "Die, you bastard! You would protect me! You would stand behind me! Die, you lying son-of-a-bitch!"

Torres had not slackened his horse's run at all. He went down the cross street, but could be heard to turn behind the main-street buildings and go south. It was later learned that one Ranger and his two-man posse chased him briefly, but remembering their orders they stopped a half mile out of town and returned.

Stephen Pendergrass lay still in the dirt. It had happened in a few seconds, so that the lawmen at the gallows had not had time to take any action. Judge Pendergrass was running in his clumsy swaying gait toward the body of his brother. The sheriff said, "He might be able to talk," and ran down the steps. He yelled back, "Whatever you do, hold Ivey! I'll be right back."

Youngblood picked up the rifle the sheriff had dropped and continued to look out for any possible further disturbance. He saw that Lieutenant Ruth was coming down from the high ground to the north west of town with his two-man posse.

Ivey had stopped his fighting for the moment. His pallor looked strange in the sunlight. It seemed to be accentuated by his black mustache and three-day growth of beard. The scar on his forehead and down into one eyebrow, which had been white against his tan, now stood out dark.

The sheriff got back at the same time that Ruth pulled up into the crowd on horseback. "Stone dead," the sheriff reported. "That damn greaser put five slugs in the middle of his chest and one in his head."

Ivey laughed harshly.

"Shall we follow the Mexican?" Ruth asked.

"Let's get this other business over with first," the sheriff said. "If I'm any judge of horses, we'll never get the Mexican anyway. He remounted the platform, took the wadded rope from his hip pocket, and tossed it to Youngblood. "Tie his legs."

Ivey began to fight again. "No, wait! You don't have to tie my legs! Damit! No!"

Youngblood had knelt to follow the instructions, but Ivey's kicking upset his balance.

"Wait! Damit! Sheriff!" the prisoner yelled, "ain't I got my last request or something? You don't have to do me this way!"

"Make your request real fast," the sheriff said.

"Don't tie my legs! You don't have to do that to me!"

The sheriff hesitated a moment, then shook his head. "They got to be tied."

Youngblood seized the upper part of the legs and worked the rope down until the prisoner could not separate his feet. Then he took another loop around the ankles and tied a hard knot. Andy and Slim were supporting all the man's weight now. Youngblood helped them support the struggling form while the sheriff put on the noose and tightened it.

The deputies released Ivey on the center of the trap

door and stepped aside. The condemned man was starting to turn, cursing, moving as well as he could with his bound feet, when the sheriff's arm crashed down on the wooden lever which released the trap. Ivey fell four feet and stopped with a snap that shook the scaffold.

His dying body writhed and jerked, though it was obvious to anyone who kept his eyes on it, from the unnatural angle of the head, that his neck was broken. Youngblood stared out across the crowd, catching the movement of the body only out of the tail of his eye. The crowd was still; most of them had their eyes averted. In the quiet, a woman's voice was loud as she sobbed, "Oh my God!" as if she had only now realized the thing that was being done. The jerking body, which later was to cause spectators recounting the event to say, "He sure had a lot of life in him," continued to move for a full minute, though it seemed to Youngblood a half an hour. When it was still, or only slightly swinging, he said to the sheriff, "You want me to try to look up the doc?"

"I don't think it's necessary," the sheriff said. "We'll give him another minute or two."

When the interminable minute or two had passed, the sheriff, his legs straddling out across the corner of the trap door, grasped the rope and cut it with his pocket knife. The body dropped in a heap on the ground.

At this time from the crowd came a sound as of air being expelled, perhaps a sigh, followed by a widespread mumbling, the sound of a hundred voices speaking low. They began to move about again. Some in the street headed back toward the center of town.

The lawmen descended to the ground. Arrangements had already been made for the care of the hanged man's body, and Youngblood was glad that he would have nothing to do with it. The sheriff looked tired as he faced them. "Lieutenant Ruth, you want to go with me?"

"Yes sir."

"I believe I'll take you too, Slim. Get us two horses. I want my paint. Andy, you better catch up a horse and run down our patrols. Tell them to come on in; it's all over."

"Let me go," Youngblood said. "Slim and I could go with the lieutenant."

150

The sheriff looked at him almost as if he had forgotten him and grinned. "No, we can handle it."

Youngblood only now sensed the full meaning in the sheriff's words, "It's all over." He had asked his superior that night a month ago, "How bad do you need me?" and the sheriff had said, "I need you real bad." But now it was all over. He felt somewhat left out until the sheriff said, "I tell you what you can do for me, Youngblood. Get off some wires on Torres. You can decide where to send them and just sign my name. And if we're not back by night, make sure Cobb feeds my stock, will you? You can tell him I said to start tearing this thing down too. He can stack the lumber in the shed."

Chapter 18

AFTER THE SHERIFF had gone, Youngblood went about his job of composing the wires and delivering them to the telegraph office. His mind was a maze of conflicting impulses and uncertainties. He wanted to run home, and yet it was only a guess on his part that the doctor had been called for Lila. He wanted to clear up the uncertainty but was reluctant too, for he could envisage only two possibilities: that was not yet time and he must wait, or else that at home he would find bad news. And he had the completely illogical feeling that he must guard the jail in the absence of the sheriff. The weeks of vigilance when his time had not been his own had left an impression that was not easy to cast off. One other thing, perhaps even yet more vague, hindered his going home: the feeling that about him still clung something of the execution he had been a part of. It had been a horrible necessity, not a thing to be ashamed of. Indeed, the whole matter, the fact that they had done their duty when it seemed impossible, was something to be proud of. Yet they had deliberately taken a man's life, and the sordid details of it stayed too fresh in his mind.

When he came back to the sheriff's office after sending the telegrams, he hunted up Elmer Cobb and set him to the task of dismantling the gallows. The little man began to tap around half-heartedly, with the obvious intention of making a week's work out of it. Youngblood took up one of his tools, a single-bit axe, and said to the little carpenter, "Stand clear." He went onto the platform and set about savagely with the butt end of the axe, knocking apart the upper structure, letting the timbers lay where they fell. Cobb stood back with eyes and mouth wide; he made low exclamations of surprise as the timbers crashed down.

The deputy worked as violently at the steps, then the boxing planks of the platform floor. He had taken up the axe, he thought, in exasperation at the lazy worker; actually he had a need to drive himself at hard physical work, even though he was already tired, as if attacking the tensions inside himself. He forgot the spectator, whose work he was doing. His mind was on his wife, who might be in pain, and on a tired sheriff riding after a fast Mexican, and on a judge, whose brother had been killed. He had eaten no lunch. It was the hottest part of the day. Still he swung the axe at the planks and timbers, sweat dripping from his clothes, until after an hour of steady work he had left no two boards together. He was almost exhausted. "Pull out the nails," he said to Elmer Cobb, "and stack it all in the shed." He slung the axe to the place where he had picked it up.

He drew water from the well, enough to fill a big wash tub in the room where he had been sleeping with Andy and Slim. Then he bathed, removing the head bandage and taking care to get all the dried blood from the back of his neck. He put on fresh clothes and headed home.

He paused at the low swinging gate in front of his house, and all that was conscious in him was like part of a prayer. Then as if in answer the simple little sound came. It was a thin sound, repeated and repeated, small but lusty, a baby's cry.

He almost broke the gate from its hinges and hit the porch with a clatter of boots. He checked his eagerness at the door, opening it softly. His Aunt Annie was coming out of the kitchen with her finger to her lips, "shooing" him for silence.

"Has it happened?" he asked. "How's Lila? Did Doc

come here?" He knew from his aunt's laughter that he must have a silly look on his face.

"Of course it's happened," she said. "Hours ago. And Lila's fine and so's your son. But you let her sleep a while."

But his wife's voice came from their bedroom. "Bart? Is that you?"

He went in, and they gave him a half-minute alone with his wife before they came in, his aunt and uncle. His aunt brought the tiny bundle and placed it beside the mother. He felt such relief to find that everything was all right that when the flap of sheet was spread back to show the tiny red face and the two women said it was a perfectly beautiful baby, such a statement did not seem ridiculous to him. Then they began to say, "those eyebrows, and those eyes—it's exactly like his daddy." His uncle grinned broadly and winked at him.

Charlie Moss had already brought the news about the events in town. Lila squeezed the deputy's hand, which she had held since he came in, and said, "We are very proud of you."

This didn't make much sense to him, but he found that his uncle and aunt had discussed at length with his wife the crucial situation of the lawmen in Carroll County during that month of July. Charlie Moss had been most strongly impressed with the odds the sheriff and his men had faced. Lila had put this idea, colored by her romanticism, alongside the fact that her husband had intended quitting but had stayed on to see it through, and had concluded that he was some kind of hero. The deputy only hoped that she wouldn't be too proud of him in front of other people.

His uncle was to say of it later, "Blamed if I didn't talk myself right out of a good cowhand."

He ate a snack and took a nap and was ready to go back to town to make sure Cobb had taken care of the stock. He went in to Lila and she said, "Don't quit your job right now. Think it over another week or two. You might change your mind."

The courthouse was quiet. The one pale-lit window at the opposite end of the building from the jail had a lonely aspect. Youngblood hoped that it was the window

153

of Judge Pendergrass, for into his mind had come a tantalizing, if perhaps foolish, idea and he meant to ask the judge what he thought about it. Upstairs he tapped lightly on the door from under which the lamp light came, and any answer was so long in coming that he wondered whether the light had been left burning by mistake. Then the judge opened the door.

"Come in, Youngblood," he said. "I'm glad to see you. I thought perhaps you had ridden with the others. Say, I heard a rumor. Do you have a new baby?"

"Yes sir, a boy, born this morning."

"Well, that sure is fine." The judge's face appeared deeply lined in the yellow light from the lamp which hung from the center of the ceiling. He seemed to contemplate the new baby, as if it were a quite different idea from what had been occupying his mind, and his face softened. His eyes twinkled momentarily behind the brass-rimmed spectacles. He repeated, "That sure is real fine. Will you be leaving Sheriff Bell now to work for Moss?"

Youngblood laughed. "No sir, if he'll have me, I'll stay on. I . . . well, I just changed my mind, I guess."

"I'm glad you did. The sheriff can use a man like you; in fact, you would make a good sheriff yourself some day. But, sit down. I really am glad you came by, Youngblood. I need someone to talk to a little bit. I'm a loquacious old man, you know. I don't suppose that I have much to say, but I guess I need someone to talk to worse than I have any time since . . . since I bunged up this leg of mine." He removed his glasses and rubbed both hands down across his face as if his eyes were tired and went on, "We have won, Youngblood. It's hard to realize, isn't it? But the victory is bitter to me. Bitter. It makes me feel as Brutus might have felt, wondering whether he had helped to kill a man who was really bigger than himself."

In the pause, the deputy said, "I don't see how we could have done anything different, Judge."

"No, that's a fact. I've been in circles in my thinking tonight and I always come back to that; we couldn't have done anything different. Oh, if I had been a smarter man I might have seen my brother's part in it earlier, and I could have disqualified myself. But that wouldn't have been any answer. In fact, I would never have been satisfied with any results much different from what we saw

154

today. We hanged William Ivey in broad daylight on the appointed day and in the county where he did his crime. And my brother—he paid his debt as easily as even I could have wished. Surely we have strained our luck, especially me, for I am an idealist, but providence has been on our side, and we have won."

"Well, Judge," the deputy said, "it seems to me like we were lucky, but we fought them pretty hard, too. I figure we hung Ivey in broad daylight because that's the way you said it was going to be."

"Yes, I like that attitude," the judge said. "But, you know, many men have tried to have their way with Stephen Pendergrass and William Ivey in the past, and they have failed. They'll say at my brother's funeral that he was a good man. He wasn't. He wasn't even a good boy; he was a child of a wild time and a wild place. He and Ivey were both like that, and more than that; they were powerful instruments of the times. You know, Torres was one of them too. We may never know where he fitted in, but we know he rode with Ivey in the past, and today he took revenge for Ivey as if he were his brother. So it is true that the ways my brother lived for the the same ways that killed him. But Stephen was more than a child, Youngblood, and more than an instrument. He is the reality of the past, which is the only thing the future can be built on. That brings me around in one of my circles, back to Julius Ceasar again. Did you ever read how Caesar led his legions to fight in Gaul, that is in France, and in Switzerland, Belgium, England, Germany? Caesar wasn't a good man, but the civilization of Europe has, down at its deepest foundation, Caesar, whether he were good or bad. And there is irony in the small stature of some of the men who stabbed him.

"You know my brother asked me once, where this courthouse would be if it weren't for him. He might as well have asked where would Comanche Wells be, for it wouldn't be here."

Youngblood wanted to object in some manner, but he didn't know how strongly the judge might have been attached to Stephen Pendergrass. He wanted to say, 'between you and your brother, the best man has won.' He wanted to tell him that the sheriff had said he'd rather have that little judge on his side than six good gun hands. He wanted to say, 'your big-shot brother, with all the advantage on his side, acted like a fool and led the men who trusted him to death and defeat.' But he couldn't put it into words and still be sure that he wouldn't offend.

"Well," the judge went on, "I've been sitting here spouting fancy yap-yap, signifying nothing, and I must get to packing. I have to gather up my books and junk and be all ready. After my brother is buried, I have a stage to catch." He sat without moving, in spite of his words. "I have a new term of court to begin—rustling, shooting, horse thieving, assorted mayhem." He chuckled and his face brightened as if he had succeeded in convincing himself that it was his part as a judge to experience all these many human failings and difficulties, remaining detached and objective, and that *this* month in Comanche Wells was such as all the others; but he succeeded only briefly and then the weight of his personal sorrow descended again on him.

"How little we know, Youngblood," he said, "of the nearness of the evil around us: It can stand right beside us, while we blindly peer into the distance. But I don't want to start on that again. Did you come to see me for any special reason?"

"Yes, I did, Judge. I sort of have a question to ask you."

"Shoot," the older man said. "If I don't know the answer, I'll say so."

"I don't hardly know how to begin. How old were you, Judge, when you started out to study law?"

"Twenty-eight. Why do you ask?"

"I'm twenty-eight. Do you think it would be silly for me to want to study law? I mean, reckon I would stand a chance?"

The judge laughed in delight. "Are you serious?"

"Yes sir. I know it's pretty silly."

"Well, I certainly don't think it's silly. It all depends on you. Did you finish the school here in Comanche Wells?"

"Yes sir."

The judge was happier than he had been all night. "I'll tell you what I'll do, Youngblood. When I come back for my next term of court I'll bring you some books. You read them and then we'll see what you think. I just believe you can do anything you set your mind to, and I'll help you every way I can."

Voices from the street and from the direction of the jail caused Youngblood to guess that the sheriff had returned. He rose and shook the judge's hand. The older man followed him to the door and clapped him on the back in affection as he went out.

He found the sheriff, Ruth, and Slim holding their horses in front of the office. The sheriff answered his unspoken question. "Torres is out of the county and into the mountains. And we wasn't gaining on him. What in the heck are you hanging around here for? You ain't even on the payroll now."

"I want to talk to you about that, tomorrow when you have time," Youngblood told him.

"I got time right now."

"Well, I want to stay on as a deputy, if you could use me."

The sheriff laughed. "Aw, I guess we could use you maybe. How come you to have a change of heart?"

"I don't know. Different things, I guess. I got me a new baby boy today."

He heard their congratulations, then took their horses and unsaddled them and headed home. That night he slept in peaceful exhaustion and did not awake until the middle of the following morning.

He came into the room where Lila was with the new child and saw her, not in bed as he had expected, but sitting beside it in a straight chair, absorbed in the task of folding a bunch of small white baby clothes.

"What in the world are you doing out of bed?" he asked.

She laughed, and it seemed like music to him. "Why I'm taking care of our baby."

"You have somebody to take care of the baby. You get back in bed."

She looked up at him and said simply, "But I want to take care of him myself."

Repetition of the words "the baby" and "our baby" jarred on his consciousness, and he did not know what the trouble was at first, then he said suddenly, "Goodnight, Lila! What's his name? I don't even know his name."

She laughed again. "Poor little feller. I thought it would be a girl, and I was going to name it Victoria, after the queen of England; but since it's a boy, he'll have to get along on whatever his papa can think up."

He put his hands on her shoulders and stood there trying to think of the great people of the world, someone who like the queen of England was worthy of giving a name to their child. When finally the name "Albert" occurred to him he was not thinking of a German prince, but of a little district judge with one game leg, and he thought the name would be a good one for a boy to wear.

Benjamin Capps was born in Dundee, Texas in 1922. He grew up on the land, the son of a working cowboy who rode horseback to a one-room schoolhouse for his elementary education. He attended Texas Technological College in 1939. During the Second World War he was in the U.S. Army Air Corps and served in the Pacific theater. After discharge, Capps returned to pursue higher education, obtaining a bachelor's degree in 1948 and a masters degree in 1949 from the University of Texas. For the next few years he taught English and journalism at Northeastern State College in Tahlequah, Oklahoma, before changing his course in life entirely, entering industry as a tool-and-die maker, at which trade he worked for the next decade while he wrote Western fiction.

Capps' first published literary effort was *Hanging at Comanche Wells* (1962), a paperback original that was never reprinted until it was published in a new hardcover edition by Chivers Press, Ltd., in 2001. *The Trail to Ogallala* (1964) followed, the story of a cattle drive from Texas to Nebraska. This novel won a Spur Award from the Western Writers of America, as did Capps' next novel, *Sam Chance* (1965) as well as his much later short story collection, *Tales of the Southwest* (1991). Virtually all of Capps' Western novels and stories depict with ambivalence the struggle for survival on the Western frontier. Later novels tend to focus unforgettably on the lives of American Indians, such as *A Woman of the People* (1966) and *The White Man's Road* (1969), the latter an unusually grim, albeit wholly realistic, view of reservation life among the Comanches. Capps' Western stories display such uniform mastery that they cannot so much be analyzed as they must be experienced. One of the author's recurring themes is how the American Indian tended to live by visions whereas the Anglo-American most often lived by dreams, and how in various, sometimes bitterly painful ways, these visions and dreams would clash with physical and social reality. *Mesquite Country* is Benjamin Capps' most recent novel.